Wilkie Collins

Miss Gwilt

A Drama in Five Acts

Wilkie Collins

Miss Gwilt
A Drama in Five Acts

ISBN/EAN: 9783337376857

Printed in Europe, USA, Canada, Australia, Japan

Cover: Foto ©Andreas Hilbeck / pixelio.de

More available books at **www.hansebooks.com**

MISS GWILT:

A DRAMA IN FIVE ACTS.

(ALTERED FROM THE NOVEL OF "ARMADALE.")

BY

WILKIE COLLINS.

(Printed for performance in the theatre only. Not published.)

———

1875.

PERSONS OF THE DRAMA.

ALLAN ARMADALE.
MIDWINTER.
MAJOR MILROY.
DOCTOR DOWNWARD.
CAPTAIN MANUEL.
MR. DARCH.
ABRAHAM SAGE.
FRANCIS.
A TRADESMAN'S LAD.
THE MAYOR AND CORPORATION OF THORPE-
    AMBROSE, SERVANTS, POLICEMEN IN PLAIN
    CLOTHES.

MISS GWILT.
MISS MILROY.
LOUISA.

NOTE.—The stage directions, "Right' and "Left," refer to the right and left of the actor as he fronts the audience.

MISS GWILT.

———◆———

ACT I.—THE GOVERNESS.

SCENE.—*The Park at Thorpe-Ambrose. On the actor's right the paling and garden gate leading to* MAJOR MILROY'S *cottage. Entrances to the stage through the trees at the back and by a shrubbery path on the actor's left. Garden seats placed here and there among the trees.* MAJOR MILROY *and* MISS MILROY *are discovered seated at a rustic table.* MISS M. *is making a nosegay. The* MAJOR *has a newspaper in his hand. He is absorbed over his reading, and is perpetually interrupted by questions from his daughter.*

MISS M.

Papa! has anybody answered your advertisement for a governess for me?

MAJOR M.

My dear, I told you this morning that a governess had answered the advertisement.

MISS M.

Has she given you a good reference?

MAJOR M.

An excellent reference.

MISS M.

What is her name?

MAJOR M.

Miss Gwilt.

MISS M.

I don't like her name, to begin with. Is she an old woman?

MAJOR M.

No.

MISS M.

Is she a young woman?

MAJOR M.

Yes.

MISS M.

Where did she live last ?

MAJOR M.

Bless my soul ! what a number of questions ! Are you to manage this matter ? or am I ?

MISS M.

I had rather we neither of us managed it. The fact is, papa, I don't want a governess at all.

MAJOR M.

Then you must go to school.

MISS M.

I don't want to go to school either.

MAJOR M.

My dear ! pray be reasonable, if it is only for a minute ! You know that I am not a rich man. The one thing I can give you is a good education. Choose for yourself, between an education at home and an education at school.

MISS M.

Choose ? Do you suppose that I could be happy for a moment out of my own dear little room at the cottage ?

MAJOR M.

In other words, you choose the governess—and there is an end of the matter. As for your little room at the cottage, my dear, I only hope it may not be some other young lady's little room before long.

MISS M.

What do you mean ?

MAJOR M.

Our cottage belongs to the owner of the Thorpe-Ambrose estate, and our lease expires next month.

MISS M.

Well ?

MAJOR M.

Well, the death of our old landlord, Mr. Blanchard, has transferred the Thorpe-Ambrose estates into the hands of a stranger. (MR. DARCH *appears at the back*.) And that stranger may not choose to renew our lease.

MR. D. (*advancing*).

Make your mind easy, Major. I answer for his renewing your lease.

MAJOR M.

You, Mr. Darch! Why, I thought you were entirely unacquainted with our new landlord, like all the rest of us?

MR. D.

I have been in correspondence with him, Major. It was my business to inform the new heir, Mr. Allan Armadale, of the inheritance to which he has succeeded. He has appointed me his lawyer, and, take my word for it, he will renew your lease.

MISS M.

Is our new landlord a young man, Mr. Darch?

MR. D.

A very young man, Miss Milroy.

MISS M.

Handsome and agreeable, Mr. Darch?

MR. D.

I must leave you to judge for yourself, Miss Milroy. I have not seen him.

MAJOR M. (*to* MR. DARCH).

One word on the subject of our late landlord. All we have heard here is that Mr. Blanchard died unexpectedly in London. Do you know how it happened?

MR. D.

It happened in this way. Mr. Blanchard was in London on business, and was a passenger on board one of the river steamers——

MAJOR M. (*interrupting him*).

Drowned?

MR. D.

On the contrary, he was the means of saving a person who might have been drowned but for *him*. A woman among the passengers threw herself overboard. (MAJOR MILROY *and* MISS MILROY *both start.*) Mr. Blanchard jumped into the river and rescued her. They were both brought on shore safely to the nearest police station. The woman soon recovered her senses, thanks to the readiness of a young man who witnessed the accident and who ran for the nearest doctor.

MISS M.

Was the young man Mr. Armadale?

MR. D.

Certainly not. The young man's name was reported to be Midwinter.

MISS M.

Midwinter? What an extraordinary name!

MAJOR M. (*interposing*).

My dear! we have still to hear about Mr. Blanchard's death.

MR. D.

Mr. Blanchard might have been alive at this moment if he had been wise enough to get into a warm bath and send for dry clothes. The medical man who had been called in—a certain Dr. Downward—gave him that advice. Mr. Blanchard laughed at Dr. Downward—and went home in a cab. The next day he was too ill to attend the examination before the magistrates. A fortnight afterwards he was a dead man.

MAJOR M.

Is it known who the woman was?

MR. D.

Nobody knows who she was. The name she gave at the examination was evidently assumed.

MAJOR M.

And this attempted suicide, on the part of a perfect stranger—— ?

MR. D.

Has made Mr. Armadale (through his mother) possessor of the Thorpe-Ambrose estates.

Enter DR. DOWNWARD. *His grey hair is parted in the middle, and falls to his shoulders. He wears a large " turn-down collar," a long, black frock-coat, and a broad-brimmed hat. His whole exterior announces an assumption of patriarchal simplicity. His manner is smoothly benevolent. He looks at everybody with the same bland smile.*

DR. D. (*addressing a servant who accompanies him*).

Is that Major Milroy's residence?

THE SERVANT.

There is the Major himself, Sir.

(*The servant goes out.* DR. DOWNWARD *advances to the* MAJOR. MR. DARCH, *after a glance at the* DOCTOR, *withdraws to the back.*)

DR. D.

I think, sir, I have the honour of addressing the gentleman who advertised, under the initial "M.," for a governess in the *Times?*

MAJOR M.

I am that person, sir.

DR. D.

I am that other person whom you applied to when the governess had answered your advertisement. Miss Gwilt referred you to Doctor Downward : I am Doctor Downward.

MAJOR M.

I hardly anticipated the pleasure of *seeing* you as well as hearing from you, doctor. Have you made the journey from London to Norfolk to answer personally for Miss Gwilt ?

DR. D.

By no means ! I have been sent for professionally to a patient of mine residing in your neighbourhood, and I have brought Miss Gwilt to Norfolk with me at the request of relatives of my patient, who wish to secure her services.

MAJOR M.

I am anxious to secure her services, doctor, for my daughter here.

DR. D. (*bowing to* MISS MILROY).

Exactly ! Your application having reached Miss Gwilt first, I think it an act of justice to inform you that other persons are anxious to engage her. If you feel the least hesitation——

MAJOR M.

I feel no hesitation.

DR. D. (*resignedly*).

Very good ! Those other persons must put up with their disappointment as well as they can. I will do myself the honour of escorting Miss Gwilt to her new sphere of action. I am unhappily old enough, Miss Milroy, to acknowledge openly that I feel a deep interest in your new governess. A very painful circumstance, Major, has enabled me to be of some slight service to Miss Gwilt, and has caused me to feel an esteem for that lady which it is not in words to express. What a charming situation you have here ! The shining sun, the warbling birds, the growing grass !—such luxuries to a worn-out London doctor like me ! In an hour, Major, I shall have the pleasure of presenting Miss Gwilt. (*Exit.*)

MAJOR M.

A very agreeable man !

MISS M.

I don't at all like him, papa. Didn't his name strike you when he mentioned it ?

MAJOR M.

Of course. It was Doctor Downward who advised Mr. Blanchard to change his wet clothes.

MISS M.

And it was Doctor Downward who attended the woman who tried to drown herself. Who can she have been ?

(*Enter* ABRAHAM SAGE. SAGE *is an infirm old man.*)

MR. DARCH (*observing him*).

The head gardener at Thorpe-Ambrose! Abraham Sage, what's the matter now?

SAGE.

The matter now, Mr. Darch, is the Mayor and Corporation, and all the folk, gentle and simple, out of the town. They are asking for you, sir. There is to be speeches and fireworks, and eating and drinking, and music and dancing—all for to welcome Mr. Armadale. (*The* MAYOR *and the* TOWN COUNCIL *enter from the back, followed by the* INHABITANTS.)

THE MAYOR (*excitedly*).

Mr. Darch, I have been looking for you everywhere. I have called a public meeting, sir, and the public have responded in such numbers that there is no room big enough to hold us, except the hall at the great house. As Mr. Armadale's representative, will you allow us to meet under Mr. Armadale's roof?

MR. D.

May I ask, Mr. Mayor, what the object of the meeting is?

THE MAYOR.

The object of the meeting, sir, is to give a public welcome to Mr. Armadale on his arrival at Thorpe-Ambrose.

(*As the* MAYOR *pronounces his last words,* ALLAN *and* MIDWINTER *appear quietly among the crowd, and pass quite unnoticed—the general attention being fixed on the* MAYOR *and* MR. DARCH *—down to the front, at one extremity of the stage.*)

ALLAN (*aside to* MIDWINTER, *while the* MAYOR *and* MR. DARCH *converse in dumb show*).

"A public welcome to Mr. Armadale on his arrival at Thorpe-Ambrose"! Here is Mr. Armadale in the middle of them, and not a soul suspects who he is. Midwinter! I wouldn't have missed this for anything.

MID.

Pray be careful, Allan. These people may not understand your mad fancy for coming among them incognito, and taking them all by surprise.

ALLAN.

Hold your tongue! you're interrupting the Mayor.

THE MAYOR (*continuing his conversation with* MR. DARCH).

I repeat, sir, the public feeling of the whole neighbourhood is bent on expressing itself—through Me. (*Addressing the crowd.*) Inhabitants of Thorpe-Ambrose! are you all agreed? A public reception for Mr. Armadale?

THE CROWD.

Hear ! hear !

ALLAN (*aside*).

Not if I know it, Mr. Mayor !

THE MAYOR (*more and more excitedly*).

A public dinner to Mr. Armadale !

THE CROWD.

Hooray !

ALLAN (*aside*).

Mr. Armadale regrets to say he is engaged for that evening.

THE MAYOR.

A triumphal arch at the entrance to the town, and an address from the Mayor.

THE CROWD.

Hooray ! hooray !

THE MAYOR.

A triumphal arch at the entrance to the park, and an address from the tenantry !

ALLAN (*aside to* MIDWINTER).

A triumphal arch at the entrance to the kitchen, and an address from the cat !

MR. DARCH (*interfering*).

One word, Mr. Mayor. Are you going to hold your meeting here, in the open air ?

THE MAYOR.

I stand corrected, sir. This is highly irregular. We must proceed by formal resolutions. You grant us the use of the hall ? (MR. DARCH *bows*.) Very good. (*To the* CROWD.) Gentlemen ! Mr. Armadale's representative permits us to meet in the hall at the great house. Follow me, if you please, follow me !

(*The* MAYOR *and* MR. DARCH *go out, followed by the Town Council, by* SAGE, *and by the inhabitants.* MAJOR *and* MISS MILROY *are left at one extremity of the stage, near the cottage.* ALLAN *and* MIDWINTER, *standing aside at the back, look after the inhabitants as they go out.*)

MAJOR M. (*turning towards the cottage*).

I'll tell your mother, my dear, that your governess will be here in an hour's time.

MISS M.

And I'll make use of my liberty before the governess comes ! My nosegay from the park gardens is not completed yet. (*She takes her unfinished nosegay from the garden table, and stops the*

MAJOR *on his way into the cottage. At the same moment* ALLAN *and* MIDWINTER *descend the stage again.*) While you are about it, don't forget to tell mamma that Mr. Armadale will sign our lease. (MAJOR M. *nods to her, and goes into the cottage.* MISS M. *turns, and sees* ALLAN *and* MIDWINTER *looking at her.*) Who can those young men be?

ALLAN (*to* MIDWINTER).
A pretty girl! I'll make acquaintance with her.

MID.
Allan! what are you thinking of?

ALLAN (*approaching* MISS M., *and taking off his hat*).
I beg your pardon, I am quite a stranger here. May I ask if I am trespassing in Mr. Armadale's park?

MISS M. (*coldly and stiffly*).
The park is open, sir, to everybody.

ALLAN.
Very kind of the proprietor, I'm sure. I beg your pardon again—I think you said something just now about Mr. Armadale signing a lease? Take my word for it, he'll sign anything you like with the greatest pleasure.

MISS M. (*haughtily*).
What have *you* to do, sir, with our lease ; And how can *you* presume to say whether Mr. Armadale will sign it or not?

(*She goes out indignantly at the back of the stage.*)

ALLAN (*to* MIDWINTER).
That's good, isn't it? You look out of spirits, Midwinter. Does this sort of thing bore you? It amuses *me*.

MID.
My dear Allan, it is time this frolic of yours was ended. There are serious duties connected with the wealth that has fallen into your hands. Pardon me for saying it, you sadly want somebody——

ALLAN.
Somebody with a steadier head than mine to keep me straight? I quite agree with you. And what's more, I've found the man.

MID.
Where is he?

ALLAN.
Here to be sure! (*He puts his hand on* MIDWINTER's *shoulder.*) You're the man.

MID.
My dear Allan! I am little better than a stranger to you!

ALLAN.

Pooh! pooh! I know all about you.

MID. (*starting back in alarm*).

You know all about me! When did I tell you—— ?

ALLAN.

I wanted no telling, the thing explained itself. How did I first hear of you? I heard of your being found insensible at the roadside near my old home. How did I first see you? Helpless at the village inn—raving in a brain fever, with nobody but strangers near you. What did I find out about you, when we had to search your knapsack? I found out that you had been an usher at a school, and that the brutes had turned you adrift in the world when your illness began. I nursed you through your illness, and I have taken a fancy to you, and there's an end of it. Let's drop the subject.

MID. (*with deep feeling*).

No! One of us must go on with the subject. You have treated me like a brother, and I have never given you my confidence in return. My life has been a very sad one: there is only that excuse for me. I lost my mother when I was quite young. My father went abroad and left me among strangers. I was starved and ill-treated. It ended in my running away. Still a mere child, I found myself one evening in the wild north of Scotland, lost on a moor. Do you think I was afraid? Not I! I had won my liberty, and I hadn't a friend in the world to regret. I laid down, alone in the dark, under the lee of a rock, the happiest boy in all Scotland.

ALLAN.

Don't talk in that way! I don't like to hear it!

MID.

When I awoke next morning, I found a sturdy old man with a fiddle on one side of me, and two dancing dogs on the other. The fiddler gave me a good breakfast out of his knapsack, and let me romp with the dogs. I was an active little boy, and he saw his way to making use of me. "Now, my man!" he said, "listen to me. You have had a good breakfast. If you want a good dinner, jump up and earn it, along with the dogs!" He led the way; the dogs trotted after him, and I trotted after the dogs.

ALLAN.

Who was the fellow with the fiddle?

MID.

A half-bred gipsy, a drunkard, a ruffian, and a thief—and, until I met you, the best friend I ever had.

ALLAN (*astonished*).

The best friend you ever had !

MID.

Isn't a man your friend who gives you your food, your shelter, and your education ? My gipsy-master taught me to walk on stilts, and to sing songs to his fiddle. We roamed the country and performed at fairs. The dogs and I lived together, ate and drank and slept together. I can't think of those poor little four-footed brothers of mine, even now, without a choking in the throat. Many is the beating we three took together—many is the hard days' dancing we did together—many is the night we have slept together, and whimpered together, on the cold hill-side. I'm not trying to distress you, Allan ; I'm only telling you the truth. The life was a life that fitted me ; and the half-bred gipsy—ruffian as he was—was a ruffian that I liked.

ALLAN.

A man who beat you !

MID.

Didn't I tell you just now that l lived with the dogs ? Did you ever hear of a dog who liked his master the less for beating him ? I served *my* master for nearly eight years. He died one day, drunk, on the moor, and I was thrown on the world again. An old lady took a fancy to me next, and tried me under the upper servants in the house. Yes; you have been friendly with a man who once wore a livery. I have seen something of Society—I have helped to fill its stomach and to black its boots. One day some money was missing. I had never even seen the money ; but I was the only servant without a character—and out I went ! My next employer was a bookseller in a country town.

ALLAN.

Come, that sounds better ! Did you find your way to a friend at last ?

MID.

I found my way to the most merciless miser in all England. He had starved everybody out of his employment when he met with *me*. I lived in his service—I educated myself with his books—for three years. At the end of that time the miser died. I was his creditor for a month's salary, and he refused me a character on his deathbed unless I promised to forgive him the debt. I bought my character on those terms. "Aha !" he whispered to me, with his last breath, "I have got *you* cheap !" Was my gipsy-master's stick as cruel as that ? I think not. A day or two after, an advertisement told me that an usher was wanted at a school. The mean terms offered encouraged me to apply, and I got the place. What happened to me next you know better than I do. The thread of my story is all wound off. My vaga-

bond life stands stripped of its mystery, and you know the worst
of me at last.

ALLAN.

Midwinter, give me your hand! Accept the steward's place,
and be my friend for life!

MID. (*deeply affected*).

Allan! Allan! I am used to harsh words and cold looks—I
am *not* used to this. Oh, if I could only feel sure of being of
some real service to you!

ALLAN.

I feel sure of it—and that's enough. Hush! there's somebody coming. (*They both draw back a little.*)

MISS MILROY (*speaking outside*).

You old wretch! Touch one of my flowers if you dare!

(*She enters on the right, holding up her dress filled with flowers,
and followed by* ABRAHAM SAGE, *with his rake in his hand.*)

SAGE.

It's no use, Miss—the flowers in the park garden are under
my charge, and must not be picked. What would Mr. Armadale say?

MISS M. (*half angry, half crying*).

If Mr. Armadale is the gentleman I take him for, he would
say, "Come into my garden, Miss Milroy, as often as you like,
and take as many nosegays as you please."

ALLAN (*advancing*).

"Come into my garden, Miss Milroy, as often as you like,
and take as many nosegays as you please!"

MISS M.

That man again! How dare you mock me in that way, sir?
Who are you?

ALLAN.

I'll make a clean breast of it to *you*, Miss Milroy. I'm Allan
Armadale! (ABRAHAM SAGE *takes off his hat, and waits for an
opportunity of speaking.*)

MISS M. (*thunderstruck*).

Mr. Armadale! (*Drops the flowers, and clasps her hands in
despair.*) Oh, heavens! I shall sink into the earth!

ALLAN.

Suppose we pick up the flowers first? (*He kneels and puts
the flowers back into* MISS MILROY'S *lap.*)

SAGE.

I bid you humbly welcome to Thorpe-Ambrose, sir. My
name is Abraham Sage. I have been head gardener here for

forty years, and my late employer had the highest opinion of me.

(*Neither* ALLAN *nor* MISS MILROY *notice* SAGE. MISS MILROY *is ashamed to receive the flowers, and* ALLAN *insists on putting them back into her dress.* SAGE *waits immovably for his next opportunity.*)

MISS M.

Don't, Mr. Armadale—pray don't! I'm so ashamed of the things I said to you. My tongue ran away with me—it did indeed! What *must* you think of me?

ALLAN (*putting the last flower back, and rising to his feet*).

I think you're the prettiest girl I've met with for many a long day. I beg your pardon, Miss Milroy. *My* tongue ran away with me that time.

SAGE (*seeing his next opportunity*).

My name, sir, is Abraham Sage. I've been employed in the grounds for forty years——

ALLAN.

You shall be employed for forty years more, if you'll only hold your tongue and take yourself off. (SAGE *never stirs.*) Well?

SAGE.

I should wish to speak to you, sir, on the subject of my son. My son has been employed in the grounds for twenty years. He is strictly sober. He is remarkably industrious. And he belongs to the Church of England, without encumbrances. (ALLAN *makes a gesture of impatience.*) I humbly thank you, in my son's name and in my own. I'll go to the house now and tell them all that Mr. Armadale is here.

ALLAN.

You will do nothing of the kind, Mr. Sage. When the time comes I'll tell them myself.

SAGE (*going out*).

I couldn't think of letting you do it, sir. Don't you be afraid of my legs! They're shaky to look at, I grant you. Never you fear—my legs will take me as far as the house.   (*Exit*).

ALLAN (*to* MIDWINTER, *who has remained at the back*).

Midwinter! Stop that old fool! (MIDWINTER *laughs, makes a sign in the affirmative, and follows* SAGE. ALLAN *turns to* MISS M.) That gentleman is my new steward, Miss Milroy, and my best friend. Come into the garden and get some more flowers. (*He gives* MISS MILROY *his arm.*) Which is the way?

MISS M. (*laughing*).

Fancy your asking your way about your own grounds! (*Suddenly drawing back from* ALLAN.) Stop! I had forgotten that horrid Miss Gwilt! Mr. Armadale, my new governess is coming to-day. I must wait at home to receive her.

ALLAN.

She hasn't come yet. Just a little stroll. Give me a faint notion of my own property!

MISS M.

Impossible! If I don't go in directly, papa will be coming out to look for me. (*The* MAJOR *appears at the door of the cottage.*) Here he is. Papa, a surprise for you. This is Mr. Armadale.

MAJOR M.

Mr. Armadale! I had no idea you had arrived at Thorpe Ambrose already. Pray come into my little cottage. The luncheon is on the table. Will you waive all ceremony, and join us?

ALLAN.

With the greatest pleasure, Major Milroy!

MISS M.

Papa, the key of the cellar. I'm butler, Mr. Armadale. We've got a little sherry, and a little claret, and a *very* little champagne. Which wine will you have? Please say champagne!

MAJOR M. (*laughing*).

If you ever have a daughter of your own, Mr. Armadale, don't begin as I have done by letting her have her own way. (*He gives* MISS M. *the key. Enter* MIDWINTER *at the back.*)

MID. (*to* ALLAN).

It was useless to speak to that obstinate old man. I have been myself to the house, and I have explained everything to the Mayor. A little civility from you will soon set things right again.

ALLAN.

See what an invaluable steward you are already! (*He turns to* MAJOR MILROY.) Major Milroy, let me introduce my friend, Mr. Midwinter.

MAJOR M.

Will you lunch with us at the cottage, Mr. Midwinter?

MID.

Pray excuse me, sir. I have a letter to read——

ALLAN (*interrupting him*).

All right! Get done with it as soon as you can, and join us at the Major's table. (*Giving his arm to* MISS MILROY.) Now for the champagne!

B

(ALLAN, MISS MILROY, *and* MAJOR MILROY *enter the cottage*)

MID.

Alone at last! (*He takes a letter from his pocket.*) What does this mean ? I find it waiting for me—forwarded from my London lodgings—when I enter Allan's house for the first time. (*He opens the envelope, and takes out a letter and a sealed enclosure which he finds inside. He places the enclosure on the table, and reads the letter first.*) " Sir,—I have only to-day discovered your address in London, thanks to Dr. Downward." (*He speaks.*) Doctor Downward ? Ah, yes! the first doctor whom I found at home when the lady was saved from drowning. (*He reads.*) " I had occasion not long since to consult the doctor profession-ally. In the course of conversation he mentioned a case of attempted drowning to which he had been called in, and I became thus informed that your address was to be found in the records of the police court as witness in the case." (*He speaks.*) Quite true! How often I have thought of that beautiful woman since ! (*He reads.*) " The object of my letter is to inform you, as your father's executor, of your father's death abroad." (*He speaks.*) Dead! And we have been strangers to one another since I was a child ! (*He reads.*) " You will receive the income which you inherit from your father, on applying at the enclosed address."

(*Enter* ALLAN *from the cottage.*)

ALLAN.

Hav'nt you done ? We are all waiting for you.

MID.

Pray don't wait ; I can't join you yet. I will be with you later.

ALLAN.

Don't be long. (*He returns to the cottage.*)

MID. (*resuming his reading*).

Where did I leave off ? Here it is ! (*He reads.*) . . . . " on applying at the enclosed address. Be pleased, in signing the necessary receipts, to sign your family name." (*He speaks.*) My family name ? What does he mean ? (*He reads.*) " Your rightful name, concealed by your father for some reason un-known to all his friends, is—Allan Armadale ! " (*He starts back, thunderstruck.*) Am I dreaming in broad daylight ? Am I mad ? *My* name " Allan Armadale ! " *My* name the same as my friend's ! (*He turns as if to enter the cottage, then checks himself.*) No ! Let me finish the letter first. (*He reads.*) " The sealed letter enclosed in this was found among your father's papers. I forward it, as you see, unopened, and remain your obedient servant." The sealed letter may solve the mystery. Where did I put it? (*He takes the letter from the table, breaks the seal, seats himself at the table and reads.*) " My son ! I have left you among strangers, under a false name. These lines, written on my deathbed, will tell you why. You are a cousin of Allan Armadale, of Thorpe-Ambrose; his father and I were brothers." (*He speaks.*) Brothers! Allan's father and my father brothers! Oh, what a discovery, for Allan as well as for me ! (*He reads.*) " You and your cousin were both christened by the name of a wealthy member of our family, whose favour we were alike interested in trying to gain. So you come by the name I leave you—Christian name and surname the same as your cousin's." (*He speaks.*) Now I understand it—Christian name and surname the same as Allan's. (*He reads.*) " My confession must follow these explanatory words: It is the confession of a crime." (*He speaks.*) A crime ! Dare I read any further ? (*He reads.*) " While you and your cousin were still infants, a mortal quarrel divided my brother and myself. Of the cause I shall say nothing ; it was equally disgraceful to him and to me. We were both husbands ; we were both fathers at the time. Friends and relatives will tell you that my brother died, at the period of the quarrel, by an accident. To you alone I confess it—that accident was the work of my hand." (*He starts to his feet shuddering.*) Oh, God ! I see it now. The one friend I have made in the solitude of my life, is the son of the man who died by my father's hand, and that man his own brother ! Horrible ! horrible ! Let me get to the end ! (*He reads.*) " Why do I darken your young life at its outset with the shadow of your father's crime ? Because the fear is on me that *you* may pay the penalty of the crime. It is written that the sins of the father shall be visited on the children. I tremble for what may happen if you and your cousin ever meet. Hide yourself from him in the future, as I have hidden you from him in the past—under your assumed name. Put the mountains and the seas between you and the other Allan. Never let the two Armadales meet in this world—never ! never ! never !" (*A pause. He folds the letter and speaks.*) Put the mountains and the seas between me and the man to whom I owe the first happiness of my life. (*He places the letter in the breast of his coat, and looks towards the cottage ; his grief overpowering him while he looks.*) Dearest of cousins, first and last of friends, farewell ! (*He turns towards the back of the stage. A pause before he speaks again.*) Must I leave him ? (*He returns towards the cottage.*) Why may I not atone for my father's crime by giving him the service of my life ? Trouble may be coming to him, and I may avert it. Danger may lie in his path, and I may be the man who saves him! (*His head sinks on his breast ; he stands thinking. ALLAN appears at the door of the cottage.*)

ALLAN (*a little exhilarated by wine*).

Midwinter, why don't you come in and taste the Major's champagne?

(*He approaches* MIDWINTER, *and puts his hand on his friend's shoulder.*)

MID. (*shrinking from him*).

Don't touch me!

ALLAN (*in astonishment*).

Have I offended you?

MID. (*sorrowfully*).

Offended me! Oh, my poor boy, are you to blame for being kind to me? And am I to blame for feeling your kindness thankfully?

ALLAN (*becoming serious on his side*).

What does he mean? Midwinter, you talk strangely—you look dreadfully pale. Are you ill? Come into the cottage. A glass of wine will put you right again.

MID.

Not now! not now! I shall soon be better. I have been considering, Allan, about the employment that you offered me. Let me go. I am not the man for the steward's place.

ALLAN.

Don't excite yourself! You shall have the place, *because* you are not the man for it. There are one or two other places in England filled on that principle. Drop this, Midwinter, or you will really distress me. Ask the Major what he thinks. The Major has been talking to me about you. He told me that a wealthy position was a dangerous position for a man of my age. "You may want a friend's advice," he said; "you may need a friend's help sooner than you think." If the Major is right, it is your advice I shall want, and your help I may need. (*He turns to enter the cottage.*) Come along!

MID. (*aside*).

My own thought reflected in *his* mind! recalled to me by *his* lips! Is it a warning to me to stay?

ALLAN (*at the cottage gate*).

Come! come! The Major is waiting to see you.

(MIDWINTER *declines by a gesture, and walks aside among the trees at the back. At the same moment* MAJOR MILROY *and* MISS MILROY *appear at the gate.*)

MAJOR M.

Anything wrong, Mr. Armadale?

ALLAN.

My friend is not very well, Major. He leaves me to make his apologies to you and Miss Milroy.

(*While* ALLAN *is speaking,* DR. DOWNWARD *appears at the back of the stage, on the left, with* MISS GWILT *on his arm.* MISS MILROY *sees them over her father's shoulder.*)

MISS M.

Papa, the new governess!

(*The* MAJOR *advances, and is presented by the* DOCTOR *to* MISS GWILT. MISS MILROY *hangs back near* ALLAN.)

ALLAN (*looking at Miss* GWILT).

By Jove! what a handsome woman!

MISS M. (*overhearing him*).

I can't congratulate you on your taste, Mr. Armadale.

MAJOR M. (*beckoning to his daughter*).

My dear, come and be introduced to Miss Gwilt.

(MISS MILROY *advances unwillingly, remaining on* MISS GWILT'S *right.* DR. DOWNWARD *occupies* MAJOR MILROY'S *place, on* MISS GWILT'S *left, which the* MAJOR *leaves vacant after introducing his daughter.* MISS GWILT *takes* MISS MILROY *kindly by the hand.*)

MISS GWILT.

The first minute or two with strangers is always a little trying, Miss Milroy; is it not? I hope I don't look very formidable? I am almost as nervous on occasions like these as you are; but I try to hide it.

MISS M. (*satirically*).

And I think you succeed, Miss Gwilt.

MISS G. (*assuming the same tone on her side*).

Do you, really? What a nice, frank, open nature you have, my dear! (*She notices* ALLAN, *and addresses the* MAJOR.) Another member of your family, Major Milroy?

MAJOR M. (*crossing to the right to present* ALLAN).

No, no, Miss Gwilt. The enviable possessor of this beautiful place—Mr. Allan Armadale.

(MISS G. *looks at* ALLAN *and bows formally, as if her first impression of him was not favourable.*)

ALLAN.

I hope I shall have the pleasure of showing you the place, Miss Gwilt (*aside*), as soon as I know anything about it myself. (*He calls.*) Midwinter!

(MIDWINTER *descends the stage.* MISS GWILT *speaks aside with*
MISS MILROY.)

DR. D. (*to himself*).
Midwinter ?   The man with the assumed name—the man the
executor mèntioned to me in London !

ALLAN (*to* MIDWINTER).
My dear fellow ! which is the way to my house ?

(MIDWINTER *smiles, and speaks with* ALLAN, *pointing to the trees at
the back.* MAJOR MILROY *addresses his daughter*)

MAJOR M.
Your governess may wish to see her room, my dear.   You
will find my little cottage furnished very simply, Miss Gwilt.
This way !

(*He holds open the gate for* MISS GWILT *to pass through. She looks
towards* ALLAN, *who is still speaking with* MIDWINTER, *as she
passes the gate.* MIDWINTER *sees her for the first time, recognises
her, and starts violently. The* DOCTOR *watches him attentively.*)

MID.
SHE here ! ! !

ALLAN (*noticing the change in him*).
What's the matter ?   You've brightened up !   Your colour
has come back ; you look like yourself again !   (*He follows the
direction of* MIDWINTER'S *eyes;* MISS GWILT *at the same moment
passing through the gate, and lingering in view, while she speaks to*
MISS M., *and admires the flowers.* ALLAN *continues aside to*
MIDWINTER.)   Ah, she's a fine woman, isn't she ?   I say ! do
you still think of leaving me, old fellow ?   Which is it now ?   Do
you go or stay ?

MID. (*with his eyes fixed spellbound on* MISS GWILT).
I stay !

THE END OF THE FIRST ACT.

ACT II.—The Doctor.

Scene.—*The interior of the fishing-house at Thorpe-Ambrose, divided by a vertical partition—with a door in it—into two rooms of unequal size. The larger of the two opens on a terrace and verandah at the back of the stage, commanding a view of a sheet of water. This room is fitted up as a museum, and is decorated with Indian and Chinese curiosities, fishing implements, ancient and modern weapons, models of ships and boats, and in a prominent place a model of a schooner-yacht.*

The smaller room (fitted up as a reading-room) is entered by a door in the partition. The upper part of the door is of glass, covered by a curtain on the side of the reading-room. Newspapers, periodicals, and writing materials are on the table. A window large enough for a man to climb through is in the wall of the room, at the back.

At the rise of the curtain Major Milroy, Miss Milroy, *and* Miss Gwilt *are discovered in the museum.* Miss Gwilt *is seated at one end of the room making a water-colour drawing of a Chinese figure. The* Major *stands looking over her.* Miss Milroy *is alone at the opposite end of the room, examining a book of engravings.*

MAJOR M.

Miss Gwilt, you are the most universally-gifted person I have ever met with. If my reckoning is right, you have been a resident in our family for something like three weeks. I declare hardly a day has passed without our finding some fresh accomplishment of yours to admire! Neelie! why don't you come and look at Miss Gwilt's drawing?

MISS M.

I am looking at the works of Raphael, papa. Perhaps I may be excused if I have no admiration to spare, even for Miss Gwilt.

MISS G.

I am charmed to find, my dear, that you are making some progress in your knowledge of art. It is something to have discovered that Raphael was a better painter than I am !

MAJOR M. (*looking about him*).

What do you think of our young squire's fishing-house, Miss Gwilt ? I confess I don't appreciate some of Mr. Armadale's curiosities. What can he want with these models of ships, for instance ?

MISS M.

Mr. Armadale has the true English love of the sea, papa. He is going for a cruise in the Mediterranean this autumn. That (*pointing to it*) is the model of the yacht which is to be built for him under his own directions.

MAJOR M.

Every one to his taste. The Indian things are the prettiest things here, to my thinking. (*He looks over* MISS GWILT'S *shoulder.*) How well you are getting on with your drawing, Miss Gwilt ! How well you do everything ! Were you educated in England ?

MISS G.

Partly in England and partly in France. My poor mother's small resources were heavily taxed, Major, for my sake.

MAJOR M.

The sacrifice has not been without its reward, Miss Gwilt. It has made you the accomplished woman you are now.

MISS G. (*smiling sadly*).

It has done more than that. It has made me feel keenly my dependent position in the world. I have had the training of a lady—for the life of a servant ! My mind has been cultivated, my tastes have been refined—and all for what ? To see people without mind and without taste prosperous and happy—to find my poverty degrading all that is highest and best in me to the level of something to sell, something which the insolence of wealth can purchase on its own terms. Don't think me un- grateful ! I am speaking of the time before you knew me. Will the day ever come when I shall deserve your kindness ? Shall I stay with you long enough to win a sister's place in my pupil's heart ?

MISS M.

You are very good, Miss Gwilt. If you stayed here a hun- dred years I should never forget you were my governess !

MAJOR M.

Neelie, that is a very improper answer to make to Miss Gwilt.

MISS G. (*to the* MAJOR).

Pray don't notice it ! *You* understand me, don't you ?

MAJOR M.

I understand, and thank you. It is really a question, Miss

Gwilt—at your age and with your attractions—whether I have
any right to keep you buried in this obscure place. A brilliant
future may be awaiting you.

MISS G. (*going on with her drawing*).
You are very kind, Major. I have no faith in the future.

MAJOR M.
No faith in the future ! Your worthy friend, Dr. Downward,
doesn't take *that* view of your prospects, I am sure. I was sorry
he had to hurry back to London on the day when he introduced
you to us. Is there any chance of our soon seeing the Doctor
again ?

MISS G.
Yes. He speaks of paying another visit to his patient in
Norfolk, and of coming here afterwards to see me in my new
home.

MAJOR M.
I am delighted to hear it. When you have told the good
Doctor all your news, I may have something to tell him on my
side in which your interests are concerned. (*Smiling, and lower-
ing his voice.*) There are younger men than I am in this neighbourhood who have the taste to admire you. There is one
young gentleman whose daily walks take him wonderfully often
in the direction of my cottage. Aha ! you understand *now ?*

MISS G. (*aside, in alarm*).
Does he mean Midwinter ?

MISS M. (*aside, in alarm*).
Does he mean Allan ?

MAJOR M.
Look into the future, Miss Gwilt, and you may see the lady
who is soon to be mistress of this great estate !

(*He walks up the stage towards the door.*)

MISS G. (*aside, with an air of relief*).
He means Armadale !

MISS M. (*aside*).
How *can* papa be so blind ? Is it possible he doesn't see
that Allan comes to the cottage for *me ?*

MAJOR M. (*returning*).
Neelie ! didn't you tell me you wanted to see the nets drawn
this morning, and the fish taken out of the lake ?

MISS M.
Yes, papa.

MAJOR M.
Come with me, then. I see the gamekeeper and his men

getting into the boat. (*To* MISS G.) Look more cheerfully at your prospects, Miss Gwilt. I say no more!

(THE MAJOR *and* MISS M. *go out.* MISS G. *puts aside her drawing materials, rises, and walks irritably up and down the room.*)

MISS G.

My position becomes more insupportable every day. The insolence of Miss Milroy; the blindness of her father to what is going on under his own eyes; the utter impossibility of my marrying Armadale, as Doctor Downward had planned—everything is at cross purposes, everything is going wrong! I wish I was hundreds of miles from this place! I wish I had been left dead at the bottom of the river! (*Pauses.*) Strange! whenever I am most reckless, whenever I am most wretched now—the thought of that friend of Armadale's comes and softens me. Midwinter! I am thinking of Midwinter again! Have I a heart still left? and has that man touched it?

(MIDWINTER *appears at the verandah.*)

MID.

Miss Gwilt, may I hope that I am not intruding on you? I have something to tell you this morning, and I hardly know how to approach the subject.

MISS G. (*smiling*).

Am I so very terrible?

MID.

You are the kindest and gentlest of women!

MISS G. (*aside*).

What is it that speaks to me in his voice?—what is it that looks at me in his eyes? (*To* MID.) You seem agitated. Has anything vexed you this morning?

MID.

I have parted this morning from something very precious to me. I have thought it right, in case of accidents, to destroy your letter—the only letter you have ever written to me.

MISS G.

My letter? Ah, yes! I wrote to thank you for your merciful silence about me in this place. You have told nobody here that I am the woman whom you saw charged at the police-station with an attempt on her life.

MID.

As a favour to *me*, don't, pray don't, speak of it again!

MISS G.

I dare not ask myself what you must think of me. I can

claim your pity, and I can claim no more! (*She leaves him dejectedly, and seats herself in a corner of the room.*)

MID.

For God's sake, Miss Gwilt, believe that you inspire me with a feeling worthier of you than pity! My heart bleeds for you! my heart longs for you! (*He kneels at her feet.*) I have dared to love you! (*A pause.*) With the first love I have ever known —with the last love I shall ever feel! Have I offended you?

MISS G.

Should I remain here if you had offended me? I am only sorry; not for myself—for *you*.

MID.

For me?

MISS G.

I have suffered as few women suffer. My life has been wasted already! You are at the beginning of *your* life. What misfortunes can *you* have known?

MID.

I have known no happiness till the day when Allan Armadale found me friendless at the village inn. Oh, Miss Gwilt! the new feeling that you have roused in my heart does not make Allan less dear to me. I see Allan as my brother when I see *you* as my wife. The love that you inspire is a noble love. It takes nothing from me which is due to others; it leaves me grateful as ever, and true as ever, to my first friend. Give me one look of encouragement! Let me hope!

MISS G.

Hope? Do you ask me to be your wife—knowing no more of me than you know now?

MID.

Let me know that you love me, and I know enough.

MISS G.

Have you forgotten how we first met? Have you never asked yourself —— ?

MID.

I have asked myself nothing that could give you a moment's pain.

MISS G. (*to herself*).

Oh, my past life! my past life! I was dreaming that I loved him. How cruelly he has awakened me! (*To* MID.) Rise, I entreat you. I cannot answer you now. Give me time to think.

MID. (*rising, and seating himself by her*).

Are you not your own mistress? (*A pause.* MISS G. *makes no answer.* MIDWINTER *takes her hand, and proceeds.*) Forgive me, if I press the question. Is there any obstacle in the way?

(DR. DOWNWARD *appears silently under the verandah. Neither*
         MISS G. *nor* MID. *observe him.*)

MISS G. (to MID.).

Pray don't press me to-day. I'm nervous—I'm out of spirits
—I'm not well.

DR. D. (advancing).

Can I be—medically—of any use? (MISS G. *and* MID. *both
start.* MID. *crosses to the opposite side of the room. The* DOCTOR
advances benignantly towards MISS G.) A little nervous, my
child? The heat of this fine summer weather! I always carry
a bottle of smelling-salts for ladies' use. Try it, my dear girl,
try it! (*He gives the smelling-bottle to* MISS G., *looks furtively
towards* MIDWINTER, *and speaks aside.*) I'll get rid of Mr. Midwinter to begin with. (*Approaching* MIDWINTER.) Good
morning, my dear Sir. Heavenly weather, is it not? How
beautiful the country is when the sun is shining, and the birds
are singing, and the grass is green! They told me at the
cottage I should find Major Milroy here. Where is he?

MID.

They are netting the fish, Doctor, at the other end of the
lake. The Major and Miss Milroy have gone to see the nets
drawn.

DR. D.

To see the nets drawn means, I presume, to see the fish die?
—die, on this heavenly day! As a matter of fact, how sad!
As a matter of cookery, how necessary! I am not a sporting
man, Mr. Midwinter. Death in any form is—medically—
abhorrent to me. I think I'll wait here until the expiring
struggles of our watery fellow-creatures are over. I can eat a
fish with infinite relish, but I can *not* see a fish die. Would you
mind telling the Major?

MID. (*after looking towards* MISS G., *who makes a sign to him to go*).

I will tell the Major with pleasure. (*In a whisper as he passes*
MISS G.) I love you!   (*Exit*).

DR. D. (aside).

Now for Miss Gwilt! (*Seating himself by her.*) Better, my
child? Have you done with the smelling-bottle? (*Takes it
from her.*) That's right! Now tell me all your news. Are you
happy here?

MISS G. (absently, as if thinking of MID.).

I am not happy.

DR. D.

Not happy! Look at the sun, my child! Look at the
birds! Look at the grass—and don't, don't take life on the
gloomy side!

MISS G. (*impatiently*).

There is no disguising it, Doctor. Your plan for restoring me to my lost place in the world—your scheme for marrying me to Mr. Armadale—has failed.

DR. D. (*shocked*).

My "scheme"? What a word to use! Scheming implies something cunning and wicked. Am *I* cunning? Am *I* wicked?

MISS G. (*sincerely believing in him*).

You know that I do you justice. I thank you for offering me the chance of becoming Mrs. Armadale. It is a chance that I have lost. We must give it up.

DR. D. (*honestly scandalised*).

Give it up? Mr. Armadale's rental reaches ten thousand a year. Mr. Armadale's widow has an income secured to her on the estate of two thousand a year. All this is at the disposal of my adopted child; and my adopted child says "Give it up" without a word of regret!

MISS G.

I can't regret not marrying Armadale. I dislike him—I distrust him—I'm afraid of him!

DR. D.

May I ask why?

MISS G.

I told you, Doctor, when we first met. My mother was the unhappy cause of a fatal quarrel between two brothers, and one of them was Armadale's father. (*She shudders with superstitious dread.*) I'm afraid! I'm afraid!

DR. D. (*walking aside and speaking to himself*).

And the other—if I am rightly informed—was Midwinter's father. Something may come of this. (*He returns abruptly to* Miss G.) My dear girl, don't let us waste our precious time in mystifying each other. Suppose we speak out plainly? When I came into this room I found you alone with Mr. Midwinter, and I thought I saw your hand in his.

MISS G. (*rising, and trying to change the subject*).

How are you getting on, Doctor, with your business in London? You were occupied with two new speculations when I last saw you. You were starting a newspaper, and you were going to open a Sanatorium. Is the newspaper getting on?

DR. D. (*ironically*).

The newspaper is deaf for the present to your kind inquiries. (*Suddenly changing his tone.*) Are you in love with Midwinter?

MISS G. (*persisting*).

Are you making money by the Sanatorium?

DR. D. (*side*).

Damn her obstinacy! I am a ruined man if I haven't got the handling of Armadale's money in three months' time! (*To* MISS G., *throwing aside all restraint*.) Do you know what you are doing? You are turning your back on your own interests— you are destroying your own prospects. You are in love with Midwinter!

MISS G. (*appealing to the* DOCTOR).

Don't blame me till you hear what I have to say. I can't resist the sympathy which draws me to that man! I am like a prisoner who feels the sun, I am like a drowning wretch who rises to the air, when I am with *him !* He thrills me with the noblest thoughts; he reconciles me to my better self; he lifts me above the atmosphere of meanness and misery in which I have stifled so long! Can you wonder that I love him? Oh, Doctor, Doctor, don't expect too much of me! I'm only a woman, after all! (*She hides her face in her hands and bursts into tears.*)

DR. D. (*resuming his fatherly manner*).

And women are occasionally hysterical, my dear. Try the smelling-bottle again.

MISS G.

I know I have offended you.

DR. D.

No; you have only surprised me. After your sad experience of the delusions of love, and the perfidy of man; after the rash attempt on your own life that followed——

MISS G. (*interrupting him with a low cry of despair*).

Oh!

DR. D.

Pardon me for recalling the painful remembrances of the past.

MISS G.

You don't recall them. It all came back upon me in its bitterness and its shame when Midwinter asked me to be his wife.

DR. D.

Bitterness? shame? You talk as if there was no excuse for you! Remember that I once knew the scoundrel who betrayed your trust in him. With my personal experience of Captain Manuel——

MISS. G. (*in sudden alarm*).

Where is he now?

DR. D. (*affecting not to understand her*).

Captain Manuel? Late of the Brazilian Navy?

MISS G.

Yes!

DR. D.

Make your mind easy. He is out of the country. (*Aside.*) He is waiting for me behind the fishing-house at this moment, and I am afraid I shall want him! (*To* MISS G.) My dear girl, let me appeal for the last time to your better sense. The golden opportunity of your life is before you. Pause before you throw it away!

MISS. G. (*irritably*).

Armadale again?

DR. D. (*persuasively*).

Ten thousand a year, my sweet friend, while he lives. Two thousand a year to his widow when he dies.

MISS G.

Oh, Doctor! Doctor! you force me to tell you everything. There is no contending against impossibilities. Armadale is privately engaged to Miss Milroy.

DR. D. (*thunderstruck*).

Engaged to Miss Milroy? Nonsense! It can't be.

MISS G.

It *is*. I know it.

DR. D.

Does Major Milroy know it?

MISS G.

Certainly not! Major Milroy believes that Armadale is in love with *me*.

DR. D. (*walking aside in triumph*).

The game is not lost yet! The Major shall know of his daughter's engagement. Where is he? (*He turns towards the door and confronts* MAJOR MILROY *and* MISS MILROY, *who enter at the same moment.*)

MAJOR M.

Dr. Downward? Welcome to Thorpe-Ambrose! How long have you been here?

DR. D.

I have visited my patient, Major, and I have been gossiping with Miss Gwilt. (MISS GWILT *slowly withdraws into the reading-room, and takes up a newspaper.* DR. DOWNWARD *addresses* MISS MILROY.) And how is this dear young lady? Ah, I needn't ask. She is as bright as the sun, Major; she is as happy as the birds; she is as fresh as the grass. Thank you, my child—thank you, for feasting an old Doctor's eyes on the charming spectacle of youth, beauty, and health!

MAJOR M. (*laughing*).

Hush! hush! Doctor! You'll turn her head.

MISS M. (*aside*).
He turn my head! Fawning old wretch! I hate a patriarch in a coat and trousers!

DR. D.
What news of our friends here, Major? How is the happy possessor of this beautiful place?

MAJOR M.
I have some news for you in that quarter, Doctor. (*He looks significantly after* MISS G., *and lowers his voice.*) Mr. Armadale is in love!

DR. D.
Natural enough at his age. (*He bows pointedly to* MISS MILROY, *who turns aside in confusion and alarm.*) The fair object of his devotion, Major, is not far to seek.

MAJOR M. (*astonished*).
My daughter? Why, she was only sixteen last birthday. Absurd!

MISS M. (*faintly*).
Papa—I'm not very well—I'll go back to the house.

DR. D. (*aside*).
I've done it!

MAJOR M. (*stopping her*).
My dear, if you are ill here is the doctor. (*To* DR. D.) Do *you* understand this?

DR. D.
My dear sir, surely it's plain enough. (*To* MISS M.) There is only one excuse for my blunder, Miss Milroy. Your father was the first to mention Mr. Armadale's name.

MAJOR M. (*sternly*).
What!

MISS M. (*bursting into tears*).
Oh, papa, papa! forgive me! Allan would have spoken to you if you had only waited a little longer.

MAJOR M.
Allan? She speaks of Mr. Armadale by his Christian name! (*Calling.*) Miss Gwilt! (MISS G. *advances from the reading-room.*) Have you seen anything going on between my daughter and Mr. Armadale?

MISS G.
I am not in your daughter's secrets, Major Milroy.

MAJOR M.
I asked you a question, Miss Gwilt.

MISS G. (*haughtily*).
I have answered your question, sir.

MISS M. (*rousing her courage*).

Don't ask Miss Gwilt, papa! If I have done wrong, I can own it, without Miss Gwilt coming between us. (MISS G. *turns away contemptuously*.) Mr. Armadale made me an offer in the garden last week, and—and I did'nt say No.

MAJOR M. (*indignantly*).

And I hear of it now for the first time!—hear of it by an accident!

MISS M.

It's my fault, papa. Allan proposed speaking to you; and I said, " No! I shall be sent to school if you do."

MAJOR M.

Mr. Armadale shall answer it to me before another hour is over his head.

DR. D. (*looking towards the verandah*).

Mr. Armadale is here.

(*Enter* ALLAN, *followed by* MIDWINTER. ALLAN *advances to the front.* MIDWINTER *remains at the back with* MISS GWILT.)

ALLAN.

Good morning, Doctor! Good morning, Major! Good morning, ladies! I'm delighted to see you all in my little museum. Major! you have heard me talk of my yacht? Come here, and I'll explain the model to you. (*The* MAJOR *looks sternly at* ALLAN, *without moving*.) What's the matter? What's wrong with Miss Milroy?

MAJOR M.

I don't know what the code of honour may be, Mr. Arma-dale, in the world in which *you* have lived. In the world in which *I* have lived, a man who visits at another man's house, and who entraps his daughter into a private engagement, is a man who has betrayed a trust that has been placed in him. Consider yourself, if you please, a stranger to me and to my daughter from this time forth. (*He turns to go. The* DOCTOR, *standing apart, rubs his hands in triumph*.)

ALLAN.

Stop a minute, Major. If I deserve harsh words, you have the consolation of knowing that you have given me my deserts. I own I have done wrong, and I ask your pardon with all my heart. But I can't resign Miss Milroy. Treat me as you may, I shall still aspire to the honour of winning your daughter's hand.

DR. D. (*aside, looking at the* MAJOR).

He has shaken the Major!

MISS M. (*to her father*).

Break *my* heart if you like, papa; but give Allan another chance!

C

MAJOR M. (*hesitating*).
Does he deserve a chance ?

MISS M.
Yes, papa, I have studied his character, and I ought to
know.

MAJOR M. (*smiling*).
You are a little fool !

MISS M. (*humbly*).
I am anything you like, papa !

DR. D. (*aside*).
The game's lost !

(*He turns his back on the rest, and stands absorbed in his own
thoughts.*)

MAJOR M. (*to* ALLAN).
I don't give you back the confidence which you have
forfeited, Mr. Armadale. I offer you a chance of recovering it,
on certain terms. I require you to abstain, for one year, from
all communication with my daughter. If, at the end of that
time, you and she are of the same mind, I will receive you as a
suitor for Miss Milroy's hand. (ALLAN *at a sign from* MISS M.
bows in silent submission to MAJOR M.'S *proposal. The* MAJOR
gives MISS M. *his arm.*) Come, Neelie !

MISS G. (*stepping forward*).
One moment, Major Milroy. (*The* MAJOR *waits.*) Your
daughter has failed in politeness to me on more than one
occasion, and I have excused her in consideration of her youth.
But my forbearance has its limits. When you questioned me
just now you looked and spoke as if you doubted me.

MAJOR M.
I only doubt, Miss Gwilt, whether I might not have placed
the care of my daughter in more experienced hands.

MISS G. (*haughtily*).
I will afford you the opportunity, sir, of trying the experi-
ment. After what has passed, I beg to withdraw from the
position which I hold in your house.

MAJOR M.
As you please, Miss Gwilt. Now, Neelie ! (*The* MAJOR
gives his daughter his arm.)

MISS M. (*in a whisper as they pass* ALLAN).
Submit, for my sake !

(*The* MAJOR *and* MISS M. *go out.* ALLAN *follows them to the door,
and looks after them.* MIDWINTER *watches his opportunity of
speaking to* MISS GWILT).

MISS G. (*to the* DOCTOR).

I should have died if I had not spoken! He looked at me as if I was his servant! (*The* DOCTOR *bows absently. Failing to rouse him from his thoughts,* MISS GWILT *turns away.* MIDWINTER *advances to meet her. They walk aside together, while the* DOCTOR *speaks his next words.* ALLAN *turns from the door, and joins them when the* DOCTOR *is silent.*)

DR. D. (*left alone in front*).

She has lost the last chance of marrying the heir of Thorpe-Ambrose! The handling of Armadale's money means the handling of his widow's income *now*. I must employ Captain Manuel. I am forced back on a crime.

(*He remains absorbed in his thoughts.*)

ALLAN (*joining* MIDWINTER *and* MISS G.).

What am I to do now? I have seen the last of my darling Neelie for a whole year. I can't stop here after that—the place is hateful to me! Let's go to Cowes to-morrow, Midwinter, and hire the first yacht that's ready for sea. (DR. D. *is roused by* ALLAN'S *voice. He looks round and listens.*) We'll cruise in the Mediterranean, and get through the time in that way. I'll go and tell the servants to pack our things and shut up the house. (*He is going;* MIDWINTER *stops him.*)

MID.

Wait a little, Allan. I have something to say to you first.

ALLAN.

All right. I'll be back in ten minutes. (*He goes out.* MIDWINTER *and* MISS G. *remain at the back, talking together.*)

DR. D. (*still pursuing his thoughts alone in front*).

Armadale goes to the Mediterranean, and Midwinter marries Miss Gwilt; the three meet abroad—and Armadale dies! On that chain of events my fortunes hang! (*He pauses, and looks round at* MIDWINTER.) The first question to settle is the question of Midwinter. Can I rely on what his father's executor told me? Is he really the other Armadale's son?

MISS G. (*hurriedly leaving* MIDWINTER, *and addressing the* DOCTOR).

Midwinter is going to speak to you. Don't answer him till you have spoken to me.

MID. (*approaching* DR. D. *on the other side*).

Dr. Downward, you stand in the place of a father to Miss Gwilt. She has resigned her situation in Major Milroy's house. In your presence I offer her a home of her own—I ask her to be my wife.

DR. D. (*looking* MIDWINTER *steadily in the face*).

In which of your two names do you ask her—Mr. Allan Armadale, the second?

(MIDWINTER *starts back, thunderstruck.*)

MISS G. (*looking at the* DOCTOR *in astonishment*).
What do you mean ?

MID. (*recovering himself*).
I don't understand you, sir.

DR. D.
Don't let us waste time and words. You are cousin and
namesake of Allan Armadale, of Thorpe-Ambrose, and you have
some reason of your own for concealing it which is unknown to
me. Your secret is safe, sir, in my hands.

MID.
Safe ! You have just revealed my secret to Miss Gwilt. I
insist on knowing why !

DR. D.
You shall hear directly. (*To* MISS G., *signing to her privately
to go into the reading-room.*) I have a letter to write. Can you find
me pen, ink, and paper in the reading-room ?

MISS G.
Certainly. (*Aside to the* DR.) Decide on nothing till I
come back. (*She goes into the reading-room. The* DR. *speaks with*
MIDWINTER. MISS G. *continues, speaking to herself.*) The other
Armadale's son ! Two of them in the second generation, as
there were two in the first ; and I, the child of the one accomplice in that story of treachery and murder, I stand here, saved
by a miracle from suicide, saved to know them both ! (*She
pauses, and absently arranges the writing materials.*)

DR. D. (*continuing the conversation with* MIDWINTER).
Just so! just so! You propose to marry my adopted
daughter. What are your means of supporting a wife ?

MID.
I have an income of my own—four hundred a year.

DR. D.
Nothing in these days !

MID.
I might add to it. In my happier moments I have aspired
to win fame and fortune by my pen. Don't laugh at my ambition.

DR. D.
I can help your ambition. A new daily paper has started in
London, and I am one of the proprietors. I might get you
tried as occasional correspondent.

MID. (*delighted*).
Oh, Doctor !

DR. D.

Are you willing to go abroad ?   Would you object to Italy—
say Naples ?

MID.

Certainly not.   But you forget Miss Gwilt.

DR. D.

I am thinking of Miss Gwilt.   If you go to Naples your
wife goes with you.

MID. (*amazed*).

You consent !

DR. D.

Hush !

(MISS G. *enters from the reading-room.*)

MISS G.

The writing materials are ready for you, Doctor.

DR. D.

Thank you, my dear. (*To* MID.) You asked me just now
why I revealed your secret to this lady.   She knows your name,
because she has a right to know it.   You have my full consent
to make her your wife.

MISS G. (*to the* DOCTOR, *reproachfully*).

Have you forgotten what I told you ?

DR. D. (*coolly*).

Completely. (*He walks aside.*)

MISS G. (*in distress and embarrassment*).

What can I say ?

MID. (*in a whisper*).

Say you love me !

MISS G. (*losing her self-control as* MIDWINTER *looks at her*).

You know I love you !

DR. D. (*returning to them and addressing* MIDWINTER).

One word more on the subject of your name.   You must
lawfully marry my adopted child.   In plainer words, you must
marry her in your own name.

MID.

In the name of Allan Armadale ?

DR. D.

In the name of Allan Armadale, and in my presence as a
witness.

MID. (*appealing to* MISS G.).

May the marriage be private ?

MISS G.

I should prefer it in private.

MID. (*to* DR. D.).

I will marry Miss Gwilt in my own name, and in your presence as a witness.

DR. D.

What about the name when you are man and wife ?

MID. (*earnestly*).

I must not, I dare not, acknowledge my own name. While Allan Armadale, of Thorpe-Ambrose, lives, it must be concealed from him and from everyone. (*To* MISS G.) I will tell you why, darling, when we are married. In the meantime, can you live, for my sake, under the name that I have assumed ?

MISS G. (*hesitating*).

Your request takes me by surprise.

MID.

Look at it as a matter of convenience only. If we passed in the world by the name that is my friend's as well as mine, think of the misunderstanding to which it might lead.

DR. D. (*aside, at the reading-room door, with an incontrollable burst of surprise*).

He is blundering blindfold on the very purpose that I have in view !

MID. (*continuing to* MISS G.).

Suppose Allan happened to leave this place a single man ?

DR. D. (*aside*).

He *will* leave it a single man !

MID.

And suppose a Mrs. Armadale was heard of afterwards ? People might think you had married Allan instead of me.

DR. D. (*aside*).

People will think that before you are a month older !

MID.

Suppose, again, that my friend died ?

DR. D. (*aside*).

He *will* die !

MID.

And suppose I was absent from you at the time ?

DR. D. (*aside*).

You will be absent to a dead certainty !

MID.

In that case, people, hearing of a Mrs. Armadale, might think you were Allan's widow.

DR. D. (*aside*).

And, in *that* case, she might claim the widow's income, and I might take half of it. I couldn't have described my own conspiracy in plainer terms!

MISS G. (*to* MID.).

Say no more. I see that it is necessary. I consent. (MID. *gratefully kisses her hand.*)

DR. D. (*cheerfully*).

Bless you, my children! What a comfort it is when lovers and parents understand each other! (*To* MISS G.) Is there anyone in the reading-room?

MISS G.

No one.

DR. D. (*aside*).

Now for Manuel!

(*He enters the reading-room.*)

MISS G. (*to* MID.).

Excuse me one moment! (*She follows the* DOCTOR *noiselessly. When he enters the reading-room, and turns to shut the door, he finds it already closed, and* MISS G. *confronting him.* MISS G. *addresses the* DOCTOR *with suppressed agitation.*) You have forced me into marrying him!

DR. D.

Forced you into marrying the man you love!

MISS G. (*in low, awestruck tones*).

Remember what I told you. My mother—the quarrel—the two brothers. Midwinter's father was one of them, and I only know it now. I'm afraid! I'm afraid!

DR. D.

Superstition? In a cultivated mind like yours? My child, I am astonished at you!

MISS G.

It's more than superstition, Doctor. I look back at my own past life—the guilty, miserable past. Midwinter knows nothing of it; Midwinter loves me. I am vilely deceiving him!

DR. D.

Answer me one question. Have you, or have you not, repented the past?

MISS G.

Sincerely, bitterly, Heaven knows!

DR. D.

A fault sincerely repented is a fault expunged from your life. Go back to Midwinter and make him happy!

MISS G.

Oh, Doctor! Doctor! I wish I could change consciences
with *you!*

(*She leaves the reading-room, closing the door after her, and rejoins*
MIDWINTER. DR. D. *seats himself at the table, and begins to*
write.)

MID. (*to* MISS G.).

My darling! we are alone at last.

MISS G. (*sadly*).

Have you no doubt of the future?

MID. (*putting his arm round her*).

Not the shadow of a doubt when I look at *you.*

(*He takes her to a chair, and seats himself by her, with his arm*
round her. They talk in whispers. DR. D. *speaks in the next*
room.)

DR. D.

Manuel's instructions. (*He reads to himself.*) "You are to
go to Naples, and you are to wait there for the appearance of an
English gentleman cruising in his yacht. The gentleman's
name is Armadale. You are to become acquainted with him,
you are to make yourself indispensable to him, and you are to
wait further instructions." (*He pauses and speaks.*) Suppose
there should be no time for further instructions? Suppose I
risk it, and give Manuel a hint? (*He writes, and repeats what he*
writes.) "Mr. Armadale is fond of the sea. The sea is the
fertile cause of accidents. If Mr. Armadale should unfortunately
meet with an accident"—(*he speaks the next words with a strong*
emphasis on them)—"move heaven and earth to save his precious
life." (*He folds the paper, and rises.*) That will do. Manuel
will understand what "saving his precious life" means. Where
is he now? I told him to wait among the trees, in case I wanted
him. (*He goes to the window and waves his handkerchief.* MID
speaks in the next room.)

MID.

Say you love me!

MISS G. (*smiling*).

Again?

MID.

Again and again!

MISS G. (*passionately*).

I love you!

DR. D. (*at the reading-room window, in an under tone*).

Manuel!

MANUEL (*speaking softly outside*).

Here

(The next moment he appears at the window of the reading-room, entering from the right-hand side of the stage. He is dressed in a shabby pilot-coat buttoned up to the throat; he wears old blue trousers, with tarnished gold lace down the seam; a sailor's hat on his head. Shabby as he is, he still retains the bearing of a gentleman. It is essential that he should not appear to the audience totally unworthy of MISS GWILT'S *regard. The scene between the two is played throughout in an under tone.)*

DR. D. (*to* MANUEL).

Stay where you are in case of accidents. (*He glances at the partition door.*) And speak low. We are not alone.

MANUEL (*in a foreign accent*).

You want my services?

DR. D.

Yes.

MANUEL.

And you pay me?

DR. D.

Double what I promised you in London, if you are bold enough to do what I tell you.

MANUEL.

Bold enough? Is it serious, then?

DR. D.

Most serious! (*He gives* MANUEL *the paper.*) There are your instructions, so far.

(MANUEL, *as he takes the paper, starts, looks over his left shoulder, and hurriedly climbs in at the window.*)

DR. D. (*alarmed*).

What are you about?

MANUEL.

Do you want me to be seen? Somebody outside! Somebody coming this way!

DR. D.

Hush! there are people in the next room. Read your instructions. Tell me if you understand them.

(*He lifts the curtain over the reading-room door, and looks in.* MANUEL *opens the paper, looks over it, and speaks to* DR. D., *who is still watching through the window.*)

MANUEL.

One word about this. (*He reads from the instructions.*) "The sea is the fertile cause of accidents. If Mr. Armadale should unfortunately meet with an accident, move heaven and earth to save his precious life." Does "save his precious life" mean, by the rule of contraries, "drown him like a dog"? (DR. D.

looks at him.) Thank you. I see what it means in your face.
Where is Mr. Armadale now?

(ALLAN *appears at the fishing-house door. The ringing of a bell is
heard faintly in the distance.*)

DR. D. (*pointing through the window*).
There!

(MANUEL *attempts to look through the window.* DR. D. *holds him
back until* ALLAN *appears more plainly in view.*)

ALLAN (*to* MISS G. *and* MIDWINTER).
The dinner-bell, my good friends! Midwinter, take Miss
Gwilt to the house. I will follow with the Doctor.

(MIDWINTER *and* MISS GWILT *rise and go to the door.* ALLAN
advances, and looks about him for DR. D.)

DR. D. (*to* MANUEL, *pointing out* ALLAN).
Now look at him!

MANUEL (*looking*).
Is that the man?

DR. D. (*dropping the window curtain*).
Yes!

ALLAN (*calling to* MID. *and* MISS G.).
I say! what has become of the Doctor?

MISS G.
The Doctor is writing letters in the reading-room.

(MISS G. *and* MID. *disappear.* ALLAN *crosses to the partition door,
and knocks.*)

ALLAN.
Doctor!

DR. D. (*to* MANUEL, *who turns in terror to the back window*).
Wait here till the coast is clear. (*He opens the partition door,
closes it behind him, and blandly confronts* ALLAN.) Yes, Mr.
Armadale?

ALLAN.
Dinner is ready, Doctor. Come and make one of us. Come
and see my new house.

DR. D. (*cordially*).
With the greatest pleasure, my dear sir! (*With a low bow,
leaving* ALLAN *to pass out first.*) After you, Mr. Armadale!

ALLAN.
Nonsense! You go first.

DR. D.
I couldn't think of it.

ALLAN.

Together, then ?   Will that do for you ?

DR. D.

Delighted, I am sure!   Shall we say arm in arm ?   (*He offers his arm to* ALLAN.)

ALLAN.

Oh! by all means !   Arm in arm !

(*They go out together by the fishing-house door.* MANUEL *remains listening at the partition door.*)

THE END OF THE SECOND ACT.

ACT III.—THE YACHT.

SCENE.—*The sitting-room of* MIDWINTER'S *lodgings in Naples. At the back of the stage in the centre a large open window of French construction, supposed to look out on the sea. Nothing is seen by the audience through the window but a cloudless blue sky, and the extreme horizon of the sea. A door at the side, on the right, leading into* MISS GWILT'S (MRS. MIDWINTER'S) *room. A door opposite on the left, through which the other characters enter and leave the stage. The room is large and sparely furnished in the Italian manner. The ceiling is painted with Cupids and allegorical figures. The floor is covered with matting. Grimy old pictures hang on the walls. Two statues on pedestals, and two antique chairs, stand on either side of the window, which must have no curtains. An old-fashioned sofa near the front of the stage on the right. On the left, a large empty fireplace to burn wood when used. On one side of it a piano. Above it a heavy marble mantelpiece, with ancient vases and a large clock. A mirror above the clock, in a faded Renaissance frame. At the front of the stage, on the left, a small table and two easy chairs of more modern construction than the rest of the furniture. A waste-paper basket under the table, with old newspapers crammed into it.*

At the rise of the curtain MIDWINTER *is discovered at the table on the left, writing. His wife is seated at his side with an Italian newspaper in her hand.* ALLAN, *dressed in yachting costume, lies at full length upon the large sofa on the right, smoking a cigar. The air of the Neapolitan " Tarantella " is heard outside the window, in the street beneath, the music gradually diminishing in tone until all sound of it is lost in the distance.*

Six weeks are supposed to have elapsed between the Second Act and the Third.

MIDWINTER (*to his* WIFE).

I wish these cheerful Neapolitan people were not quite so fond of their national melodies! It is no easy task, Lydia, to write news for the English public with that musical accompaniment in the street.

MISS G.

Don't write any more, love ! You have done nothing but work, work, work, for the last three days. The newspaper is making a perfect slave of you. (MIDWINTER *smiles, and looks up from his writing.*)

MID.

I think I have done at last. Stop! Have I included my extracts from the Italian newspapers?

MISS G.

Long since! The Italian newspapers are all in the waste-paper basket.

MID.

What do I see in your hand, my dear?

MISS G.

I declare I had forgotten it, though it *is* in my hand! (*Reading the title.*) " The Leghorn Gazette." Pah! the sight of it is quite enough, and the smell of it is perfectly odious! (*She stoops to throw the paper into the basket.*)

MID.

Stop! stop! I must look through it first.

MISS G. (*eagerly*).

Let me look through it for you! I will read the whole news-paper if you wish it.

MID.

There is not the least necessity, my dear, to read half of it. I always put a mark in ink against the passages that I may want to quote. If you see an ink-line on the margin anywhere, read me the marked paragraph.

MISS G. (*looking over the first page of the paper*).

No ink lines so far. (*Folding back the first page, and looking at the second.*) Here is a marked passage! Dear me, what a strange story of the loss of a ship!

ALLAN (*from the sofa*).

A ship! That interests *me.* Read it in English, Mrs. Mid-winter. I have learnt to swear in Italian, and there my acquaintance with the language ends.

MISS G. (*to* MID.).

Do *you* wish me to translate it?

MID.

Certainly, my love, if Allan wishes it.

MISS G. (*translating from the newspaper, aloud*).

" Foundering of the brig ' Speranza ' off the coast at Leghorn. —An extraordinary confession has been made in connection with the loss of this vessel by one of the crew. The man gave himself up to the police yesterday. He declares that the brig was intentionally sunk off the coast on a dark night by boring holes in the bottom of the vessel. And he adds that the captain was locked into his cabin when the crew took to the boats, and was purposely left to drown in the brig. The object of this atrocity appears to have been plunder. The captain was discovered to be in possession of a sum of money of which he had privately taken charge, and the mate and crew agreed to rob and murder him in the manner described. Further particulars will appear in our next number."

ALLAN.

Infernal scoundrels ! If you write about them, Midwinter, take a high moral tone. Say you hope they will all be hanged !

MID.

Let us be sure, Allan, that they deserve hanging first. We will wait and see what appears in the next number. (*To his* WIFE.) Fold the paper, Lydia, with the marked passage uppermost, and put it here by my desk. (*He rises and crosses to* ALLAN, *who gets up and meets him.* MISS G. *puts* MID.'s *writing materials in order.*)

ALLAN (*to* MID.).

I have got some news for you. Don't be alarmed—it isn't news for the English papers. I have settled to hire the new yacht, and somehow or other I have picked up a crew. It has been hard work to get the vessel ready for sea.

MID.

Ready for sea ! I thought the repairs were not even begun yet.

(MISS G. *leaves the writing-table and approaches* ALLAN *and* MID.)

ALLAN (*putting his hand on* MIDWINTER'S *shoulder*).

My dear fellow, you are confusing the crazy little vessel I sailed in from England, and sent back again, with the fine new yacht that I hired a week since in the port of Naples.

MISS G. (*putting* ALLAN'S *hand off* MIDWINTER'S *shoulder*).

When you have quite done with him, Mr. Armadale, perhaps you will allow *me* to say a word ?

MID. (*smiling at her petulance*).

My dear Lydia !

ALLAN (*aside*).

Mrs. Midwinter does'nt love me. Never mind. Miss Milroy

does. (*To* Miss G.) Do you believe in dreams? I dreamt of Miss Milroy last night.

MISS G. (*aside*).

He is always talking of Miss Milroy! (ALLAN *returns to the sofa, whilst* MISS G. *continues to* MID.) What shall we do to-morrow?

MID.

To-morrow? Let me see, to-morrow I must go to Capua.

MISS G.

Not without me?

MID.

Of course not!

ALLAN (*from the sofa*).

What is going on at Capua?

MID.

Excavations in the neighbourhood are going on. I have promised to send a report to the newspaper. (*To his* WIFE.) We will go to-morrow, my dear, and sleep at Capua, and come back the next day.

ALLAN.

Ah! that is just the sort of excursion Miss Milroy would like. I wish they could discover *her* at Capua!

MISS G. (*aside*).

Miss Milroy *again!* (*To* MID.) To-morrow let it be. (*Whispering.*) I want to give you a kiss. Get rid of Armadale.

MID. (*whispering back*).

Poor Allan! Have some mercy on him.

ALLAN (*from the sofa*).

How long have you been married, Midwinter?

MISS G. (*answering for her husband*).

A month to-day, Mr. Armadale.

ALLAN.

When is it customary and proper for newly-married couples to leave off whispering in the presence of a third person?

MID. (*laughing*).

Don't be severe, Allan! I confess we deserve it. (MISS G. *leaves him.*) Are you going away?

MISS G.

I may as well look out the dress I shall want for to-morrow. (*Whispering.*) Leave him, and come and help me to pack.

MID.

As much packing as you like, if you will only give me time.

I must post my letters, and I must ask at the office about con-
veyances to Capua. (*Goes to the table and remains there, addressing
and stamping his letters.*)

ALLAN (*rising*).

Talking about posting letters, I sometimes think I will write
to Mr. Darch, at Thorpe-Ambrose.

MID. (*surprised*).

Have you never written to him yet?

ALLAN.

Not a line. I left Mr. Darch in charge of everything when
I went to London with you and your wife. I got all my money
in London, and there was nothing else to write about. There
would be no reason for writing now if I wasn't so anxious for
news of Miss Milroy.

MISS G. (*aside*).

Again! The idiot can talk of nothing else!

ALLAN (*to* MISS G., *noticing her impatience*).

I hope I am not in the way here, Mrs. Midwinter? You
needn't stand on any ceremony with an old friend like me. I
only want five minutes' quiet talk with your husband.

MISS G. (*with sudden suspicion of* ALLAN'S *motives*).

Does "quiet talk," Mr. Armadale, mean talk with him in
private?

ALLAN (*speaking in his usual easy tone*).

Talk with him in private? *I* have no secrets! There is no
mystery about *me*.

(*He turns away, entirely unconscious of having given offence, and
walks towards the window.*)

MISS G. (*aside*).

He has no secrets? No mystery about *him*? He looked me
straight in the face when he said those words! What do they
mean? Has he been prying into my past life? (*To* ALLAN.) I
leave you, Mr. Armadale, to your "quiet talk" with your friend.

(*She kisses her hand to* MIDWINTER, *and goes out on the right.*)

MID. (*taking up his letters at the table*).

Are you for a walk to the post-office, Allan?

ALLAN.

I am afraid I must go back to the yacht.

MID. (*stopping on his way out.*)

The yacht? What did you tell me just now about this new
vessel of yours?

ALLAN.

I told you I had picked up a crew and got the vessel ready for sea.

MID.

An English crew?

ALLAN.

No. The English crew were all paid off before I got to Naples.

MID.

You don't mean that you have engaged a Neapolitan crew?

ALLAN.

I had no other choice. There were no Englishmen to be got. Don't you be afraid! They are dirty, but they will do. I have had the help of a most invaluable fellow in picking them out.

MID.

A foreigner?

ALLAN.

Yes.

MID.

And a stranger?

ALLAN.

Yes. He was standing by, and he saw the trouble I had in making the men understand me. He offered to interpret. Of course I accepted the offer. "You seem to know a sailor when you see him," I said. "Are you used to the sea?" "I have been used to the sea half my life," says he. One thing led to another, and when he came on board the next day he brought his testimonials with him. What do you think? It turned out that he had been a naval officer in his time!

MID.

A naval officer reduced to offer his services to you as interpreter?

ALLAN.

Oh, the poor devil has had all sorts of misfortunes! But poverty isn't a crime, you know, and testimonials speak for themselves. I am going to try him as my sailing-master.

MID.

You are going to put a perfect stranger in command of your yacht?

ALLAN.

Only on approval. I have been cautious, I can tell you! I am going to try the yacht about the bay for a couple of days, just to get her trim before the cruise. If we suit each other, it is understood that I only engage the new sailing-master after that.

D

MID. (*with sudden resolution*).
You said you were going to the yacht.   I will go with you.

ALLAN.
That's right !   But I thought you had business of your own ?

MID. (*gravely*).
My business can wait.   I want to satisfy myself that you are running no unnecessary risks.

ALLAN (*amused by his anxiety*).
Hadn't you better wrap me up in cotton wool, and put a glass case over me at once ?

MID. (*seriously*).
Allan ! do you remember the old times at Thorpe-Ambrose ?

ALLAN.
Of course I do !

MID.
When you persuaded me to stay with you, and when I accepted all that your kindness offered, I had but one advantage to offer you in return—the devotion of my life.   New interests have sprung up, new duties have claimed me, since that time. But what I promised my friend then I promised him for life. Come to the yacht !

ALLAN.
What a good fellow you are !

MID.
Shall we find the sailing-master on board ?

ALLAN.
Yes, unless we miss him in the street.   I told him to call here if he wanted to see me before I got back to the vessel.

MID.
You told him to call here !

ALLAN.
My dear fellow, he is presentable anywhere, though he *is* rather poorly dressed.   He was at the Opera last night, and he saw you and your wife in your box.   He did nothing all the evening but look at Mrs. Midwinter.   Even *you* must admit that he is a man of taste after that !

MID. (*a little impatiently*).
Did you appoint a time with him ?

ALLAN.
No.

MID.
Let us take our chance then of finding him on board.

(*Enter* MISS G. *from her room. She stands for a moment at her own door observing* MID. *and* ALLAN.)

ALLAN (*whispering to* MID.).

Your wife is jealous of me already. Don't tell her you are coming on board the yacht.

MISS G. (*aside, looking at* ALLAN).

Whispering to my husband! (*Advancing and addressing* MID.) I thought, love, you were going to ask about the con- veyances to Capua?

MID.

I am going, my dear, I am going.

MISS G.

Does Mr. Armadale accompany you?

ALLAN.

I am going on board the yacht.

MISS G. (*to* MID.).

You will come back soon?

MID.

In half an hour—in less, if I can manage it. (*He kisses her.*) Now, Allan! (*They go out together on the left.*)

MISS G. (*alone*).

What has Armadale been saying about me behind my back? Nothing, or I should have seen it in my husband's face. And yet! and yet! (*She seats herself, and pauses, thinking.*) Oh, me! is the blessed peace of mind that some women know, never to be mine again? I have tried so hard to be worthy of my hus- band! I have loved, honoured, and obeyed him! I have done all but confess to him the miserable story of the past! (*She rises, and paces backwards and forwards impatiently.*) Why does the kiss he has left on my lips burn me with the guilty sense of my own deceit? One fault—committed when I was so innocent and so young; repented so bitterly and so truly—and it pursues me like the vengeance of heaven! *Any* words may tell my husband how he has been deceived. *No* words can tell him how he is loved! I mustn't think of it! I mustn't think of it! (*She approaches the sofa, and impatiently brushes away the ashes left by* ALLAN'S *cigar.*) Armadale's filthy cigar. How I hate him! how I hate him! (*She looks round the room wearily.*) What can I do to take me out of myself? I'll play. (*As she seats herself at the piano a man's voice is heard from the street outside, singing the opening bars of the serenade in "Don Pasquale," then pausing for a moment.* MISS G. *speaks during the pause.*) Music again in the street! The opera we heard last night! (*The voice resumes and pauses again.* MISS G. *rises in sudden terror.*) The voice sounds familiar to me! There is something in it I seem to know! (*With a gesture of horror.*) Oh, no, no—impossible! I'll play— I'll play. (*She goes back to the piano, stops, suddenly rushes to the window, looks out, and returns.*) My fancy is playing me strange tricks to-day. Some idle fellow singing as he went by; and I half thought it was—— (*She stops, shuddering.*) His very name chokes me!

(*Enter* LOUISA *on the left.*)

LOUISA.

There is somebody below, ma'am, who wants to see you.

MISS G.

A lady or a gentleman?

LOUISA.

A gentleman, I suppose.

MISS G.

You suppose?

LOUISA.

A gentleman—not very well dressed.

MISS G.

Did he ask for me by name?

LOUISA.

He asked first for Mr. Armadale, and then he asked for the lady of the house.

MISS G. (*aside*).

Suspense is worse than the worst certainty. (*To* LOUISA.) Show him in.

(LOUISA *retires, holds the door open from within, and closes it after the visitor.*)

(*Enter* CAPTAIN MANUEL.)

MISS G. (*starting back with a cry*).

Manuel!

MANUEL (*coolly*).

Certainly. I announced myself to you, musically, in the street. What are you surprised at?

MISS G.

Here? In my husband's house? (*She falls into a chair.*) Oh, this is too horrible!

MANUEL.

What reception is this of a man once dear to you? An officer in the Brazilian Navy! A patriot in exile! A gentleman under a cloud! Is this my welcome? After all I have suffered too? Shameful! shameful!

MISS G.

Suffered! He talks of what he has suffered, and talks of it before *me!*

MANUEL.

Certainly before *you*. I invite the first person who passes in the street to look at me and to look at you, and then to say which has suffered most ! You are handsomer than ever, you are beautifully dressed, you are living in superb apartments, you have got (*seating himself on a chair by the table on which the newspaper lies*) one of the most heavenly chairs I ever sat in. So much for *you*. Now look at *me !* I have got hollows in my cheeks, I have got tubercles on my lungs, I am without linen—do you hear that? an officer and a patriot with nothing under *this* (*striking his breast, and melting into tears*) but a morsel of flannel, an inflamed mucous membrane, and a broken heart. And there she sits, and doesn't pity me !

MISS G.

What can I say? What can I do? Base even as I knew him to be, he is doubly degraded since I saw him last! (*To* MANUEL, *with a shudder of disgust.*) Why do you come here? I insist on knowing.

MANUEL.

I come here by appointment, to see Mr. Armadale.

MISS G. (*amazed and terrified*).

What! you and Armadale know each other?

MANUEL.

Know each other? I look on Mr. Armadale as my rich brother. I am already sailing-master of his yacht.

MISS G. (*starting to her feet in horror*).

I am a lost woman ! Armadale and my husband have gone different ways this morning. They will be together again before the day is out. What may this wretch not have told Armadale? What may Armadale not tell my husband? (*She turns furiously on* MANUEL.) Is it money you want? Have you come here to sell me your silence if I am rich, to betray me if I am poor? You have ! I see it in your face !

MANUEL.

Pardon me ! you see nothing but pulmonary consumption in my face.

MISS G.

Have you told Armadale?

MANUEL.

About what ?

MISS G.

About the past time—the time when I was mad enough to listen to you, to believe in you, to love you. (*To herself.*) That cruel smile answers me, he *has* spoken ! It was not for nothing that I suspected Armadale this morning. (*To* MANUEL.) Don't speak to me, don't drive me mad, give me time to think !

MANUEL.

With the greatest pleasure. (*He walks aside.*) I want time to think myself. I have not said one word about the past time to Armadale—I should have been a born idiot to do so. For his friend's sake he would have kicked me out of his yacht. (*He looks round at* MISS G.) Shall I tell her I have said nothing ? Bah ! quite useless ! She would not believe me on my oath. No ! no ! I shall leave her in her delusion. With this good result. She will stick at no sacrifice to keep Armadale and her husband apart ! (*To* MISS G.) Have you done thinking, my dear ? I have no concealments from *you*. I confess it. In the course of conversation I have told Mr. Armadale about you and about me.

MISS G. (*advancing on him furiously*).

Why did you tell him ? In your own vile interests why did you betray me to *him* ?

MANUEL.

Don't you see why ? Did I not hear you say just now that Armadale and your husband might be together before the day was out ? I speculate on that ! It rests with you to part those two gentlemen before the day is out.

MISS G. (*bewildered*).

It rests with me ?

MANUEL.

I am Armadale's sailing-master, and the yacht is ready for sea.

MISS G. (*seizing the idea*).

Oh ! ! !

MANUEL.

The trial trip is to be for two days at least. Use your influence over your husband—who knows your influence, you tigress in petticoats, better than I do ? Begone with your husband before Armadale comes back ! The wind is fair. One word from me, and we are off with Armadale on board !

MISS G. (*wildly*).

You want money, and I have got none !

MANUEL (*pointing to the jewels she wears*).

Does a throat like yours want a brooch to set it off ? You have a handsome bracelet there. I condemn that handsome bracelet ! It distracts my attention from the prettiest wrist in the world !

MISS G. (*piteously*).

They are my husband's keepsakes !

MANUEL.

If Armadale and your husband get together later in the day, and get talking about *me*, what sort of keepsakes will they be then ?

MISS G. (*throwing her brooch and bracelet at him*).
Take them !

MANUEL (*catching them, and uttering a cry of pain*).
The devil take you and your temper! The pin of your brooch has pricked my thumb ! (*Looking at his right hand thumb in serious alarm.*) Oh, heavens, I am bleeding ! Slight injuries to people's thumbs have been known to end in lockjaw. Look at it !

MISS G. (*to herself*).
I once trusted this abject wretch !

MANUEL.

You have thrown your miserable jewels at me as if I was a dog; you have wounded my feelings as well as my thumb. I insist on an apology—in the form of something else !

MISS G.

If I fetch my necklace, will it release me from the sight of you ?

MANUEL.

Suppose you try. (MISS G. *goes into her room.* MANUEL *puts the jewels into his pocket, pauses, feeling in his pocket, produces and opens a letter.*) What is this ? More instructions from Doctor Downward ! I am here in my own little interests. Has the Doctor any reason to complain of me for that ? Let us see. (*He reads.*) "Telegraph to me if the accident has happened at sea, and if that precious life has *not* been saved. One word— 'Drowned'—will be enough. Keep your eye on Midwinter and his wife—and count on your reward from me." It is easy enough for the Doctor to sit at home and write about Mr. Armadale's "precious life." But it is not so easy to make the accident that kills him. There *is* such a thing as capital punishment still left—in spite of the philanthropists. And *my* life is not to be trifled with! (*Puts back the letter, and looks impatiently towards* MISS GWILT'S *door.*) What a time she is ! I have no patience with a woman who does'nt know where she puts her things ! (*He takes up the newspaper from the table.*) The *Leghorn Gazette?* Any news from Leghorn ? What is this paragraph marked in ink ? "Foundering of the brig *Speranza?* " (*He reads the paragraph eagerly, and starts to his feet.*) Here is the accident, ready made to my hands ! Ten minutes work at sea to-night, will let the water into the yacht. Five minutes more, and the boat may be lowered. A turn of my hand, and Armadale will be locked into his cabin. (*He walks to and fro, fanning himself with the newspaper.*) I am in a fever when I think of it! Another vessel will spring a leak to-night, and another owner will be drowned on board!

(MISS G. *re-enters with the necklace.* MANUEL, *who has kept the newspaper in his hand thus far, now puts it back on the table.*)

MISS G. (*handing him the necklace*).

Leave me. Stop! How do I know, now you have got my jewels——?

MANUEL.

That I shall perform my part of the bargain? Look out of your window there, with your opera-glass in your hand.

MISS G.

What do you mean?

MANUEL.

Your window looks on the sea. When the yacht sails you will hear a gun fire. When you hear the gun, go to your window. I shall be at the helm—and I will take care that you see Armadale on board. Does that satisfy you?

MISS G.

Yes.

MANUEL.

Have you anything more to say to me? Suppose Armadale finds his way to your husband in the future?

MISS G.

He won't find his way to my husband. I shall take care to keep them apart.

MANUEL.

Chance may bring them together in spite of your care. Would it be worth something more if I brought you news——?

MISS G.

What news?

MANUEL.

Suppose an accident happened to Mr. Armadale? Ah, my tigress, can you prevent an accident?

MISS G.

You villain! Are you tempting me to a crime?

MANUEL.

Is a man in my state of health capable of committing a crime? Vessels have sprung leaks before now. Owners of vessels have sometimes been drowned by accident on board. Think of it, my dear. (MISS G. *recoils from him.*) Hush! I hear footsteps on the stairs!

(*Enter* MIDWINTER *and* ALLAN *on the left.*)

MISS G,
My husband ! and Armadale with him

MANUEL (*aside, to her*).
Leave it to me !

ALLAN.
Here is the Captain, after all !

MID. (*distrustfully*).
We have been looking for you, Captain Manuel.

MISS G. (*aside, glancing in terror at* MID.).
There is a change in his voice !

MANUEL (*to* MID.).
The servant showed me in, Sir, supposing Mr. Armadale to
be here. This lady was so polite as to say that I might wait
a few minutes on the chance of his coming back.
(MIDWINTER, *with his eyes fixed distrustfully on* MANUEL, *acknow-
ledges the explanation by a formal bow.*)

MISS G. (*aside, stealing another look at* MID.).
He doesn't even look at me !

ALLAN.
All right, captain—all right ! How is the wind ?
(*He takes* MANUEL *aside up the stage.* MID. *looks anxiously after
them.*)

MISS G. (*aside*).
Armadale has told him ! I shall die at his feet !

MID. (*remembering his wife, and turning to her*).
I beg your pardon, my love. How pale you look !

ALLAN (*coming down again*).
Midwinter !

MISS G. (*aside, with a sigh of relief*).
Safe—so far !

ALLAN (*to* MID.).
Famous news ! the wind is fair, and the yacht is ready to
sail.

MID.
One moment, Allan. (*Turning to his wife.*) You are not ill,
Lydia, are you ?

MISS G.
No—no ! not ill ! A little faint, that's all. I don't think
Naples agrees with me.

MID.
We will leave Naples next week. Go to your own room, my
darling, and rest a little.

ALLAN (*stopping* MISS G. *as she turns to go*).
Good bye, Mrs. Midwinter, for two days.

MISS G.

A pleasant voyage, Mr. Armadale. (*Aside.*) How he looked at me when he said "for two days!" (*She goes into her own room.*)

ALLAN.

I wish you were coming with us, Midwinter; but I must not ask a newly-married man to part from his wife. (*To* MANUEL.) If the wind holds we ought to be clear of the bay before sunset. Between this and to-morrow, captain, I expect you to make the yacht do great things.

MANUEL.

Between this and to-morrow, Mr. Armadale, I will make the yacht do things she has never done yet.

MID.

May I ask how you know what the vessel will do before you have been to sea in her?

MANUEL.

It is a habit of mine, sir, to look into the future.

ALLAN.

Is there a moon to-night?

MANUEL.

No.

ALLAN.

We must keep a bright look-out. Don't scruple to wake me if anything happens.

MANUEL.

If anything happens, Mr. Armadale, you may depend on my coming myself to your cabin door.

MID. (*to* MANUEL).

Have you ever been employed as a sailing-master before?

MANUEL.

Never.

MID.

You were formerly, I think, an officer in the Brazilian Navy?

MANUEL.

A captain in the Brazilian Navy, if you please.

MID.

Will you excuse me if I ask whether you have preserved your captain's commission?

MANUEL.

Poverty must learn, sir, to excuse everything. I know that

my shabby coat is against me. I know that the world judges by outward appearance.

MID.

Stop a minute, Captain Manuel. Considering that we have all got eyes in our heads, and that the object of eyes is to see, it would be rather wonderful if we did *not* judge by outward appearances—at any rate to begin with. As to your coat, you must permit me to say that there are men who might be dressed in the finest broadcloth that ever loom produced, and whom I would not trust with sixpence for all that.

ALLAN (*looking at* MID. *in surprise*).

He's out of temper! What for, I wonder? (*To* MANUEL.) This gentleman is my best and dearest friend. You won't object to show him your testimonials, I am sure?

MANUEL.

Show! I request permission, sir, to *overwhelm* your friend with my testimonials.

ALLAN.

All right! all right! (*Aside.*) *He's* losing his temper now!

MANUEL (*producing a bundle of papers tied with dirty ribbon, and addressing* MID. *with the air of an injured man*).

My testimonials! (*Holding up the ribbon and putting it to his lips.*) You may think this shabby. It is indescribably precious to me—it once bound a woman's hair. Ha! what memories! I wipe away a tear, and hand you my captain's commission. (MID. *carefully examines the commission.*)

ALLAN (*looking at* MANUEL).

What fun the fellow is! I wonder Midwinter can keep his countenance!

MANUEL (*to* MID.).

I wait, sir, for your objections. I pause, with an immovable sense of what is due to myself.

MID. (*handing back the commission*).

The commission is regular—I can make no objection to it.

MANUEL (*to* ALLAN).

Observe the effect of document Number One! Now for document Number Two. (*He hands it to* MID.) Testimonial of my capacity. Certificate from the Naval Bureau that I submitted to my lieutenant's examination and triumphed. I pause for the second time!

MID. (*handing the paper back after examination*).

For the second time, I have no objection to make.

MANUEL.

You have nothing more to say?

MID.

Nothing.

MANUEL.

And this is English justice! One of us must blush for the other. Let it be *me!* (*To* ALLAN.) Mr. Armadale, the wind is fair, and your yacht awaits you ready for sea. (*He withdraws to the door.*)

ALLAN (*aside*).

The sooner I part them the better. (*Approaching* MIDWINTER, *and gaily offering his hand.*) Good-bye, messmate, for a couple of days. The wind is waiting for us, and you have seen the captain's papers. (*He takes up his hat, and straps his opera-glass over his shoulder.*)

MID.

Wait a minute—wait! (*Aside.*) Stolen or forged, the fellow's papers are beyond dispute. What am I to do?

MANUEL (*from the door*).

Do you sail to-day, Mr. Armadale, with the breeze, or do you wait in port for a calm?

ALLAN (*to* MID.).

Good-bye!

MID.

Stop! I'll go down to the port and see you off.

ALLAN.

Bravo! come along!

MID.

I'll follow you in five minutes. Mind you don't sail before you see me.

ALLAN.

All right! Now, captain!

(*He goes out on the left.*)

MANUEL (*bowing ceremoniously to* MIDWINTER).

I have the honour, Sir, of wishing you a good morning, and a keener sense of human merit. (*He goes out after* ALLAN.)

MID. (*alone*).

In the name of heaven what am I to do? Allan has money with him—a large sum of money—and I saw him show it before two of the men in the cabin. If ever there were a set of ruffians on board a ship those ruffians are Allan's crew. If ever I saw a man with scoundrel written on his face, Allan's sailing-master is that man. My friend is going blindfold into danger, and going without ME! (*A pause.*) No! not without Me—cost what it may! (*Another pause.*) Oh, unsearchable Providence! has the time of atonement come at last? Am I—by saving Allan—to expiate my father's crime ? (MISS G. *opens the door of her room and looks in.*) My wife ! what am I to say to her ?

MISS G.

Has Mr. Armadale gone ?

MID. (*struggling to compose himself*).

Yes.

MISS G. (*timidly*).

Did he go to the office with you ?

MID. (*absently*).

The office ?

MISS G.

The diligence office for Capua ?

MID. (*aside*).

I have got my excuse ! (*To his wife.*) No, no ! Allan and I only met here at the door.

MISS G.

Has anything happened ? You look——

MID. (*assuming cheerfulness*).

I look embarrassed, don't I ? I have bad news for you, Lydia ; I must go to Capua alone.

MISS G.

Alone ?

MID.

I have inquired about the accommodation. There is no hotel in which an English lady could pass the night.

MISS G.

Is that all ? I care for no discomfort, darling, when I am with you. (MID. *looks uneasily at his watch.*) Why do you look at your watch ?

MID.

If I go at once I shall catch the second Diligence, and I shall be all the sooner back again with you.

MISS G.

No, no ! I can't let you go without me ! I am anxious—I am ill ! Naples is killing me. Let us leave it to-morrow, and never see it again !

MID.

I will be back in time to start for Rome to-morrow night. You can settle everything for me before I return. (*He turns away to his writing-table, and speaks aside.*) Allan will be tired of waiting for me. (*Re-opens a drawer, takes out a key, and gives it to his wife.*) Here is the key of my desk. The bills are in it, the money is in it. Courage, my darling ! Good-bye !

MISS G. (*with her arms round his neck*).

Oh, don't go without me !—don't go without me !

MID. (*disengaging himself, and placing her on a seat*).

Till to-morrow, Lydia—only till to-morrow ! (*He hurries out on the left.*)

MISS G. (*rising, and calling after him*).

Come back ! I want to speak to you. He has gone ! Is there a purpose in his leaving me ? Oh, no, no ! I saw his eyes moisten, I felt his dear arms trembling round me when he said good-bye ! Miserable creature that I am to suspect *him* of deceiving *me !* It's Armadale's fault ! It is Armadale who makes me suspect my husband. Has he sailed in his yacht ? No : I have not heard the gun fire yet. Shall we be away before he comes back ? Yes ; we start for Rome to-morrow night. (*A pause.*) It seems a strange time of day to be going to Capua ! I wonder what time the Diligence leaves ? Perhaps he may miss it—perhaps he may be obliged to come back. (*She rings the bell.* LOUISA *enters on the left.*) I want you to get me some information. Can you find out when the Diligence goes to Capua ?

LOUISA.

The landlord is downstairs, ma'am. Perhaps he may know.

MISS G.

Ask the landlord. (LOUISA *goes out.*) Can my husband have deceived me ? Has he seen some woman——? Absurd ! I am the one woman in the world to *him !* No one divides him with me but his friend—his hateful friend ! (*She accidentally disarranges some of the things on the table.*) How awkward I am ! I must make his table tidy again. (*Enter* LOUISA.)

LOUISA.

The Diligence to Capua, ma'am, goes at six in the morning.

MISS G. (*impatiently*).

You have mistaken me ! I want to know about the Diligence in the afternoon.

LOUISA.

There is only one, ma'am—the Diligence that goes in the morning.

MISS G.

The landlord must be wrong !

LOUISA.

He spoke very positively, ma'am.

MISS G.

That will do. (LOUISA *goes out.*) What should the landlord know about it ? Of course the landlord is wrong ! Those positive people generally are wrong. I wonder where the Diligence office is ? What ! distrusting him again ? I'll go and employ myself. I'll go and pack up. (*She rises and checks herself.*) No! I must put his table right first. What did he tell me about this newspaper? He said I was to put it by in his desk, with the ink mark uppermost. (*Looks for the ink-mark, and finds it.*) What is this on the margin? a stain of blood? (*Looking at it closer, more in curiosity than in alarm.*) It looks like a finger-mark in blood. Manuel! I remember my brooch pricked him! The sight of it sickens me. I'll cut it out with my scissors. What was the wretch reading when he stained the paper in this way? "Foundering of the brig *Speranza*." (*A pause. She has hitherto shown curiosity and annoyance, but no alarm. The newspaper now drops from her hand, and the first suspicion of the truth dawns on her.*) Am I dreaming? Am I mad? (*A pause.*) Was it after I saw him with the newspaper, when he spoke of vessels springing leaks and owners being drowned on board? or was it before? After! (*The whole truth bursts on her.*) If Armadale sails, he sails to his death, and I am concerned in it! (*She rings the bell violently.* LOUISA *enters with a note in her hand.*) Get a carriage instantly! I must go down to the port!

LOUISA.

A messenger has just come from the port, ma'am, and has left this note for you.

MISS G. (*snatching the note from her*).

My husband's writing! (*She reads.*) "My own Love,—I cannot reconcile it to my conscience to deceive you, even for a good end. Allan has need of me. I have gone with Allan." (*The note falls from her hand. She stands for a moment struck speechless by the discovery.*)

LOUISA (*looking at her in terror*).

My mistress! my dear mistress! (*At the sound of the servant's voice* MISS G. *suddenly rallies into action, and makes distractedly for the door.* LOUISA *follows, and holds her back.*) Where are you going, ma'am? You have not got your shawl; you have not got your hat!

MISS G. (*struggling with* LOUISA).

Let me by! I shall kill you! Let me by!

(*The muffled report of a gun is heard from the sea.* MISS G., *with a cry of horror, releases* LOUISA, *and totters a few steps towards the window. At the same moment the topsails of a schooner-yacht —no other part of the vessel being visible—are seen gliding into view through the window.*)

MISS G. (*petrified with horror*).

The yacht! the yacht!

THE END OF THE THIRD ACT.

ACT IV.

SCENE.—*The drawing-room of* MISS GWILT'S *lodgings in London.*
A door of entrance in the centre, at the back, by which visitors
enter and go out.   Other doors at the sides, right and left.
The door on the right is supposed to lead into MISS GWILT'S
room.   The drawing-room is small and modestly furnished.
Writing materials are placed on a side table.
At the rise of the curtain the stage is vacant.   A bell, from below,
is heard to ring twice.   LOUISA *enters by the door on the left.*

LOUISA.

No peace for anybody in these London lodgings !   The door-
bell is going, first for one lodger, and then for another, from
morning to night.   One ring for the first floor, two rings for the
second, and so on up to the garret.   This time it's somebody
for us.   (*She opens the door at the back.   A shop porter enters with*
a milliner's basket.)

THE PORTER.

Number twelve, Bearwood Buildings, second floor ?

LOUISA.

Quite right.   That's here.

THE PORTER (*opening his basket*).

Mourning bonnet and mourning mantle for a lady.   Paid for
at the time.   Anything for the porter, Miss ?

LOUISA.

No.   The shop charges quite enough, without paying the
porter.   (*She places the bonnet and mantle on a chair.*)   Ah, my
poor mistress ! so young and so nice-looking, and obliged to wear
this horrid black ?

THE PORTER.

Come, I say, Miss !—don't you abuse black, if you please !
It's the most becoming colour a lady can wear.

LOUISA.

What do *you* know about it ?

THE PORTER.

In our mourning warehouse, Miss, we all know about it.
There's nothing like black—let your complexion be what it may !
If you're light, black sets you off.   If you're dark, black's dark
like you.   Did you say there was nothing for the porter, Miss ?

LOUISA (*relenting*).

You are a very impudent man!

THE PORTER.

And you are a very pretty girl! And what's the natural con-
sequence? (*He kisses her in spite of her resistance. At the same
moment* DR. DOWNWARD *enters by the centre door. The* PORTER
touches his hat, and goes out. LOUISA *appeals to the* DOCTOR *in
great confusion.*)

LOUISA.

I am not to blame, if you please, sir? He's a low fellow.
I shall complain to his master!

DR. D. (*benevolently*).

My good girl, I am no saint. Young fellows will be young
fellows—and stealing kisses is the most excusable of all forms of
petty larceny. (*Changing to a tone of the deepest sympathy.*) How
is your mistress?

LOUISA.

Very poorly, sir. She hasn't had a night's unbroken rest
since the dreadful news came to her at Naples.

DR. D.

You were at Naples with her, were you not?

LOUISA.

Yes, sir. I was with her when the news came that the yacht
was lost, with every soul on board.

DR. D.

Lost, with every soul on board! I knew Mr. Armadale,
I knew Mr. Midwinter. How inexpressibly shocking! Both
drowned!

LOUISA.

Both drowned, sir.

DR. D.

Were any remains of the yacht found at sea?

LOUISA.

Yes, sir. They found some furniture floating about, and one
of the yacht's boats upside down.

DR. D.

Were any bodies found near the upset boat?

LOUISA.

Only one, sir, and that owing to his having a lifebelt on.
The doctor said he must have died of exhaustion. A storm
came up unexpectedly that night, and the life was beat out of
him, like, by the sea.

DR. D.

Was the body identified?

E

LOUISA.

Yes, sir. It was the body of the sailing-master of the yacht. (*She turns away, and re-arranges the bonnet and mantle on the chair.*)

DR. D. (*aside*).

Most satisfactory! Captain Manuel first does all I want of him, and then gets beaten to death in his lifebelt by the sea. Much obliged to the sea! (*To* LOUISA.) Has your mistress any plans for the future?

LOUISA.

My mistress thinks of living quietly at Thorpe-Ambrose. (*She approaches the side door on the right.*)

DR. D. (*aside*).

I venture to predict she will find Thorpe-Ambrose too hot to hold her! (*To* LOUISA). Are you going to your mistress's room, my good girl?

LOUISA.

Yes, sir.

DR. D.

You had better say I am here, in case she may be well enough to see me.

LOUISA.

What name, sir?

DR. D.

Doctor Downward. (LOUISA *goes out by the door on the right.*) So my fair friend persists in retiring to Thorpe-Ambrose! Have I had time to set the necessary scandal afloat before she gets there? It's a question of dates—let me look at my pocket-book. (*He produces his pocket-book, and looks back through it; then reads*). "Tenth of the month—a letter with a mourning border, from my fair friend. She is coming back to England, and she proposes to see me in London, on her way to Thorpe-Ambrose.—Eleventh of the month. Sent my fair friend's character down to Thorpe-Ambrose before her—in an anonymous letter to Major Milroy. Purport of the letter:—Major Milroy has been deceived, and Miss Milroy has been cruelly injured, by an abandoned woman. The Major supposed—as Miss Milroy supposed—that Miss Gwilt left Thorpe-Ambrose to marry Mr. Midwinter. It now appears that Miss Gwilt used poor Mr. Midwinter as a blind to hide her designs on rich Mr. Armadale. Positive proof of this statement enclosed, in the shape of a copy of the marriage certificate, showing that 'Lydia Gwilt' was married privately in London to 'Allan Armadale.'" (*He puts back the pocket-book.*) Nobody at Thorpe-Ambrose knows that there is a second "Allan Armadale," and that Midwinter is the man! The widow's income is to be had for the asking. (*He looks towards the door on the right.*) And here comes the woman who must ask for it!

(Enter MISS GWILT *from the right, dressed in widow's weeds. The rapid changes from one feeling to another which have hitherto characterised her have all disappeared. A settled depression is expressed in her manner throughout the earlier part of her interview with the* DOCTOR.)

MISS G.

Thank you, Doctor Downward, for coming to see me.

DR. D. *(taking both her hands in his).*

Oh, how sad this is ! My dear, dear lady ! My poor afflicted friend !

MISS G.

I am not ungrateful for your kindness, but I am beyond the reach of sympathy. When women are in distress, you know what a relief it is to them to cry. I have not had that relief since my husband's death. The tone you are so good as to take is useless with *me*. Sit down. I have something to say to you.

DR. D. *(aside, placing chairs).*

I don't like her language ! I don't like her looks !
(They seat themselves.)

MISS G.

I wish to consult you as a medical man. Do you detect any serious change in me since we met last?

DR. D. *(assuming his professional manner).*

Turn a little this way, if you please. More towards the light. Thank you. *(He scrutinises her face closely, feels the pulsation at her temples and her wrist, leans back in his chair and considers, then speaks again.)* Must I tell you the truth ?

MISS G.

If you please.

DR. D.

I detect serious nervous mischief since we met last. Let me write you a prescription.

MISS G.

Not now. Does nervous mischief, if it goes on long enough, sometimes end ——

DR. D.

In insanity? Yes. Don't be alarmed. There are remedies ——

MISS G.

I am not alarmed. I have been thinking of the remedy.

DR. D.

May I ask what it is ?

MISS G.

I can only tell you by returning to a subject which we once spoke of in England—Captain Manuel.

E 2

DR. D. (*assuming astonishment*).

What has the Captain to do with the object of this interview ?

MISS G.

Manuel revealed to Armadale the disgraceful secret of my life. And Armadale—I am certain of it—told my husband what Manuel told *him*. There is the thought that is driving me to madness. I have had grief to bear; I have had remorse to struggle with. I might have conquered both, but for the conviction I feel that my husband died knowing I had deceived and disgraced him. His spirit and mine are spirits separated in other spheres than this. I think of it, and think of it, and it always ends in that.

DR. D.

Nervous mischief! nervous mischief !

MISS G. (*not heeding him*).

I am hardened with a dreadful hardness. I am frozen up in a changeless despair. I feel the good that there is in me going day by day. I feel the evil gaining on me, little by little, with slow and stealthy steps. I dread myself! There is but one hope left for me. My husband's love—if he had lived—would have made me a good woman. The dear memory of him may soften and save me yet.

DR. D.

Pardon me ; on your own showing it is the memory of him that is doing you harm.

MISS G.

I can't reason—I can only feel. Doctor, I am not a bad woman. No bad woman could have loved Midwinter as I loved him. But there are seeds of evil in all mortal creatures. I am left alone with a great despair. A bad end will come of it if something is not done to touch my heart. Help me to make the best, and not the worst, of my lonely and friendless lot. Tell me if a quiet life, among old happy associations, may not help my mind back to health. If I could live at Thorpe-Ambrose, among the scenes where he first said he loved me, I might get to think differently ; I might find a refuge from myself.

DR. D.

Pardon me if I speak plainly. Wherever else you may take refuge, you can't go to Thorpe-Ambrose.

MISS G. (*wearily* .

Why not?

DR. D.

Scandal, my afflicted friend—scandal has spoken against you at Thorpe-Ambrose, and has found listeners, as usual.

MISS G. (*rousing herself*).

What do they say of me ?

DR. D.

Must I repeat it?

MISS G. (*with sudden firmness*).

I insist on your repeating it.

(*Enter* LOUISA, *with a card in her hand.*)

LOUISA.

A gentleman, ma'am, who wishes to see you.

MISS G. (*reading the card*).

" Mr. Darch, of Thorpe-Ambrose, on business from Major Milroy." (*She looks at* Dr. D.) We can't be interrupted now. Ask Mr. Darch to call again in half an hour.

DR. D. (*to* LOUISA).

Ask Mr. Darch to take a seat in the outer room. Your mistress will ring for you. (LOUISA *goes out.* DR. D. *continues to* MISS G.) Pardon me for presuming to interfere. I have a reason for what I am doing. Are you in correspondence with Major Milroy?

MISS G.

I wrote to him a day or two since to ask if a lodging could be found for me at Thorpe-Ambrose.

DR. D.

Has he answered your letter?

MISS G.

No.

DR. D.

Mr. Darch's business here may be to bring you the answer.

MISS G. (*with weary impatience*).

Can you expect me to attend to him, when you have just told me that my character is slandered, and when I am waiting to know how and why?

DR. D.

See Mr. Darch, and you will know how and why from a witness on the spot.

MISS G. (*starting*).

Do you really mean it?

DR. D.

I really mean it.

(MISS G. *rings.* LOUISA *appears.*)

MISS G.

Show Mr. Darch in.

(LOUISA *goes out.*)

DR. D.

Summon all your courage, my dear lady. You will need it; believe me, you will need it.

(*Enter* MR. DARCH, *shown in by* LOUISA, *who retires and closes the door*.)

MR. DARCH (*to* MISS G., *with a formal bow*).

You have addressed a letter, madam, to Major Milroy, of Thorpe-Ambrose?

MISS G. (*surprised at his tone*).

Yes.

MR. DARCH.

You request the Major to assist you in finding lodgings at Thorpe-Ambrose?

MISS G. (*as before*).

Yes. Will you take a seat, Mr. Darch?

MR. DARCH.

I am here in discharge of a painful duty, madam. I must beg to decline taking a seat.

MISS G. (*to* DR. D.).

Do *you* understand this?

DR. D. (*with an assumption of the deepest pity*).

Only too well, my afflicted friend—only too well!

MR. DARCH.

I have business in London, madam; and Major Milroy, acting on my suggestion, leaves it to me to answer your letter. Speaking as the Major's legal adviser, I have to express my surprise at your venturing to write to him, and I am equally at a loss to understand why you still persist in assuming the name of Midwinter.

MISS G. (*indignantly*).

"Assuming the name of Midwinter?" What do you mean, sir?

MR. DARCH (*continuing impenetrably*).

I refrain, madam, from expressing any opinion of your conduct. I merely inform you that you are known in your true character at Thorpe-Ambrose. If you persist in showing yourself there your presence will be viewed in the light of a public outrage.

DR. D. (*with his eyes on* MISS GWILT).

Oh, what language to use! What cruel, cruel language to crush a woman with!

MISS G.

The woman is *not* crushed. The woman will pay back tenfold every humiliating word which has fallen from that man's lips. (*To* MR. DARCH.) Of what am I accused, sir? Of what vile lie are you the mouthpiece?

MR. DARCH.

You will do well to profit by my warning, madam. I have no more to say. (*He turns to go*.)

MISS G.

Stop him, Doctor! That man has grossly insulted me. He shall not leave the room until I know the meaning of it.

DR. D. (*placing himself between* MR. DARCH *and the door*). Explain yourself, sir.

MR. DARCH.

I will explain myself, Dr. Downward, in the fewest and the plainest words. It is known at Thorpe-Ambrose that this lady entrapped Mr. Armadale into privately marrying her, and used Mr. Midwinter as a means to conceal her proceedings.

MISS G. (*outraged and astonished*).

Oh !!!

·MR. DARCH.

We all feel sincere sympathy for poor Miss Milroy; we all consider such conduct as I have described the conduct of an adventuress. Let me pass, sir. I have no more to say. (*He turns to go out; DR. D. bows, and draws back to let him go.*)

MISS G.

Stop! I insist on being heard.

MR. DARCH (*taking out a folded slip of paper*).

It is useless, madam, to waste time and words. There is a copy of your marriage certificate; I have myself verified it at the church. (*He lays the certificate on the table and goes out.*)

MISS G. (*to* DR. D.).

Do you expect me to submit to this? Follow him, and bring him back.

DR. D. (*resignedly taking a chair*).

My dear friend, we can't contradict him if we do bring him back. (*He opens the certificate.*) Look! There it is, in the plainest words. " Certificate of the marriage of Allan Armadale and Lydia Gwilt." Who will believe that you married Midwinter? Who can doubt that you are Armadale's widow, after such evidence as that?

MISS G.

I can prove that I married Midwinter.

DR. D.

Excuse me, you can do nothing of the kind. There is no such name as Midwinter in this certificate, and there is only one Mr. Armadale known at Thorpe-Ambrose. The facts are against you, my dear lady. You must submit.

MISS G.

Submit to be treated like the most abandoned woman living? Submit to be defamed and insulted? Do you hear? I say they have defamed and insulted me.

DR. D. (*coolly*).

Quite true.　They have defamed and insulted you.

MISS G.

The way to be even with them !　Show me the way !

DR. D.

Is it possible you don't see the way ?　Be even with them by the means which they themselves have put into your hands. Bring the wretches who have insulted you cringing to your feet ! (*Rising, and striking his hand energetically on the table.*)　Stand on your marriage certificate.　Claim the rank, and claim the income, of Armadale's widow.

MISS G. (*starting as she realises the idea*).

Oh, the daring deceit !　the splendid wickedness of it !

DR. D.

Deceit ?　Wickedness ?　I repudiate the words.　What did you say to me just now ?　Armadale told your husband the disgraceful secret of your life.　In justice to yourself, seize the compensation.　Claim the rank and claim the income of Armadale's widow.　(*He looks at his watch.*)　The post goes out in a quarter of an hour.　There is just time to make your choice.　Shall I write to Armadale's executors ?　Yes or no ?

MISS G. (*impetuously*).

Yes !　(*She points to the writing materials.* DOCTOR DOWNWARD *goes to the side table and writes rapidly, taking the certificate with him.* MISS GWILT *walks excitedly up and down the room.*)　Be quick, Doctor—be quick !　Don't let me get cool on it !　My conscience may make itself heard—my resolution may fail me.

DR. D. (*showing her his letter*).

Here is your claim on the executors, in two sentences, backed by a copy of your certificate, and attested by myself, as the witness present at the marriage.　Ring for the girl, and send her to the post.

MISS G. (*ringing*).

What next ?　what next ?

DR. D.

You shall hear when the servant has gone.　(LOUISA *enters.*) Run with this to the post, my good girl, and mind you are in time.　(LOUISA *goes out with the letter.*)　That letter will be received to-morrow morning.　You shall follow it in person, and take possession of the house—escorted by *me.*　Pack up your things, Mrs. Armadale !　We will start by the morning train. (*He leads her to the door on the right.　She suddenly stops and draws back from him.*)　What is the matter?

MISS G. (*turning towards the bell*).

Is there time to call Louisa back ?

DR. D. (*astonished*).

Call her back ?   What are you thinking of ?

MISS G. (*sadly*).

I am thinking of my dead husband.   He was the soul of honour—he abhorred deceit.   His spirit may be looking down on me at this moment.   I wish I had said No!   I wish I had said No !

DR. D.

Too late, my dear lady, to wish that.   The post-office is in the next street, and the letter is in the box by this time.

MISS G.

My mind misgives me !   I don't like it.

DR. D.

Your mind wants occupation—that's all.   (*He opens the door on the right for her*).   Occupy yourself.   Pack up !

MISS G.

I don't like it !   I don't like it !   (*She goes out slowly*).

DR. D. (*alone*).

Curious !   There is an undergrowth of goodness in that woman's nature which is too firmly rooted to be easily pulled up. I may have some trouble with her yet.   Well, the trouble must be faced.   The writs are out against me ; the money must be had ; and the one way of getting it is the way I have taken.   (*He walks up and down thinking*).   About the servant here ?   The girl was with her mistress at Naples, and the lawyers might question her.   Yes, yes !   I must find Louisa another place.   (*Enter* LOUISA).   Well, were you in time with the letter ?

LOUISA.

Yes, sir—with more than five minutes to spare.   There is a gentleman downstairs, asking if we know your address.

DR. D. (*to himself*).

Are the bailiffs after me ?

LOUISA (*continuing*).

His name is Milroy, and there is a young lady waiting for him in a cab at the door.

DR. D.

Major Milroy and his daughter !   (*He considers for a moment.*) Tell the gentleman I happen to be here on a visit, and ask him to come upstairs.   (LOUISA *goes out.*)   The enemy in our camp ! In my fair friend's interests I must draw the enemy's teeth.   (*He looks towards the door on the right.*)   Shall I tell her before he comes in ?   No.   In her present state of mind I can't trust her to face the Major.

(*Enter* MAJOR MILROY, *shown in by* LOUISA, *who closes the door and withdraws.*)

MAJOR M. (*stiffly*).

I regret to intrude upon you, Dr. Downward. Family circumstances compel me, quite unexpectedly, to make the journey to London, and to speak to you on a very painful matter.

DR. D.

Sit down, Major Milroy.

MAJOR M. (*seating himself*).

You were present at Thorpe-Ambrose, sir, when I discovered that my daughter was privately engaged to Mr. Armadale?

DR. D.

Yes.

MAJOR M.

You heard what I said on that occasion, and what Mr. Armadale said?

DR. D.

Certainly.

MAJOR M.

You were also present, if I am not misinformed, at the marriage of Mr. Armadale and Miss Gwilt?

DR. D.

I was present as the only witness.

MAJOR M.

My daughter's infatuated attachment to Mr. Armadale leaves me no alternative, sir, but to ask you a very delicate question. She positively refuses to believe in Mr. Armadale's marriage. Have you any objection to personally assure her that you saw him married to Miss Gwilt? My child's health is suffering, and I can do nothing to relieve her. I have shown her a copy of the marriage certificate (MISS MILROY *softly opens the centre door*), and she persists in disbelieving——

MISS MILROY (*advancing*).

I persist still! (DR. D. *and* MAJOR M. *both start*.) Fifty certificates wouldn't persuade me that Allan married Miss Gwilt. (DR. D. *looks anxiously towards the door of* MISS G.'s *room. The* MAJOR *speaks to his daughter*.)

MAJOR M.

Neelie, what are you doing here? You are acting most improperly. I told you to wait below in the cab.

MISS M.

I beg your pardon, papa. My patience gave way—I couldn't endure the suspense any longer.

MAJOR M.

Now you *are* here, listen to what Doctor Downward has to tell you.

MISS M. (*whispering to her father*).

I can't listen to him, papa. His face says, "Don't believe me."

MAJOR M. (*severely*).

Listen. (*To* DR. D.) Dr. Downward, you saw Mr. Armadale married to Miss Gwilt?

DR. D.

Most assuredly.

MAJOR M. (*to* MISS M.).

What do you say now?

MISS M.

What I have said all along. Allan is true to me.

(DR. D. *is struck by the last words, and listens attentively. The door of* MISS GWILT'S *room opens. She stands on the thresh-hold, unobserved by the persons present.*)

MAJOR M. (*to* MISS M.).

How can you blind yourself in this way to the plainest proof?

MISS M.

How can I do anything else, when I love Allan?

DR. D. (*interposing*).

"Allan is true to me"? "I love Allan"? Major Milroy, your daughter speaks as if Mr. Armadale was a living man.

MAJOR M. (*amazed*).

Have you not heard the news?

(MISS G. *slowly advances into the room, still unobserved.*)

DR. D. (*with a sudden misgiving of the truth*).

What news?

MISS M. (*discovering* MISS GWILT).

Papa! Papa! (*She tries vainly to draw her father's attention to* MISS G.)

MAJOR M.

There is no doubt of it, Dr. Downward. Mr. Armadale is a living man. (MISS GWILT *staggers, and catches at the nearest chair to support herself.* DR. D. *and the* MAJOR *discover her.*)

DR. D. (*to* MISS G.).

Compose yourself. It's a false report. Go back to your room, and leave it to me.

MAJOR M. (*looking at* MISS G.).

She here! Leave us, Neelie. (MISS M. *draws back, but does not leave the room.*) It is no false report, sir. The news of Mr. Armadale's rescue has forced me to follow my lawyer to London. I had a letter from Mr. Armadale this morning, asking to see my daughter, and writing as if he was still a single man.

Miss G. (*advancing slowly towards* MAJOR M., *and speaking in low, distinct tones.*)

One word, Major Milroy.   Mr. Armadale had a friend with him.

MISS M. (*in a whisper*).

Oh, papa, look at her ! look at her !

DR. D. (*cautioning the* MAJOR, *and placing himself near* MISS GWILT).
Take care what you say, sir !—take care !

MAJOR M. (*to* DR. D.).

I don't understand you.   After what I have said already why should I conceal the rest ?   Mr. Midwinter is saved with his friend.

(MISS GWILT *sinks into the* DOCTOR'S *arms, with a faint cry.*)

DR. D. (*aside*).

Damnation !   (*He places* MISS G. *in a chair, and occupies himself in restoring her.*)

MISS M. (*whispering*).

Look at him, papa—look !   Doesn't his face tell you that he is caught in a lie ?   For my sake—if you won't for Allan's—let us go to the lawyer and tell him what we have seen !

MAJOR M. (*sharing his daughter's conviction*).

She may be right !   In any case, this is no place for a young girl.   Come, Neelie !

MISS M.

To the lawyer's ?

MAJOR M.

To the lawyer's.

(*He goes out with* MISS M.   MISS G. *begins to revive.   The* DOCTOR *looks round him.*)

DR. D. (*to* MISS G.).

They have left us.   Shall I raise you in the chair ?

MISS G. (*faintly*).

Yes.   (DR. D. *raises her in the chair.*)   Did I hear it ?   Did I dream it ?   Midwinter ?   My husband ?

DR. D.

Your husband is saved from the wreck—saved to claim you, after you have declared yourself to be the widow of his friend !   There is but one chance for us—we must stick to our story now.

MISS G.

Take me away !   Hide me from him, before he comes back !

DR. D.

Hide you ?   My letter will be in the hands of Armadale's executors to-morrow morning.   If Midwinter finds his way to you there is but one alternative—you must deny him to his face !

MISS G.

I shall die at his feet if he only looks at me!

DR. D.

He won't look at you.

MISS G.

What do you mean?

DR. D.

What did you tell me yourself? Your husband knows that you have deceived and disgraced him. If you acknowledge him now (in your own words) you submit to be treated like the most abandoned woman living. Thanks to Armadale—remember that!

MISS G. (*vacantly, putting her hand to her head*).

Armadale? My head swims; my mind fails me——

DR. D.

Rouse yourself! Armadale is living to ruin us both if he is publicly confronted with *you*. (*A knock is heard at the door.*) Hush! somebody outside. Come to your room! (*He half leads, half carries her to the door of her room.*)

MISS G. (*in terror*).

Is it my husband?

DR. D.

Go in, and you shall hear. (*He opens the door on the right. She passes into the room. A second knock is heard at the centre door.*)

DR. D. (*calling*).

Come in! (ALLAN *enters hurriedly. The* DOCTOR *starts back in astonishment.*) Mr. Armadale!

ALLAN.

How are you, Doctor? Has Midwinter been here?

DR. D.

I have seen nothing of him. (*Assuming his bland manner.*) My dear sir! accept my sincere congratulations on your rescue from the sea. By what miracle did you and your friend escape drowning?

ALLAN.

No miracle, Doctor. We escaped, thanks to these clumsy shoulders of mine. The scoundrels fastened down the hatch on us before they left the yacht. Midwinter couldn't move it. I got *my* shoulders under it, and up it went. We were just in time to swim clear of the sinking vessel.

DR. D.

Can such things be? A man looks at the sun, listens to the birds, walks over the grass, and then fastens down a hatch on his brother man! Who can fathom the abysses of the human heart?

ALLAN.

There we were in the sea, Doctor, for nearly an hour. The storm in which Manuel and his ruffians were drowned in their boat was close on us when the ship picked us up.

DR. D. (*aside*).

What business had the ship to pick them up? Excessively officious on the part of the ship!

ALLAN (*continuing*).

We landed at Naples only two days after my friend's wife had started for London. We followed her back, and traced her to these lodgings. I expected to find Midwinter here. Between ourselves, Doctor, I'm afraid there's something wrong about that handsome wife of his.

DR. D.

You astonish me!

ALLAN.

Captain Manuel had certainly some grudge against Midwinter. The scoundrel slipped a letter under Midwinter's cabin door before the yacht sank. From the time my friend read that letter he has never once spoken to me about his wife.

DR. D.

Bless my soul!

ALLAN.

It's all guess-work, mind. Manuel never ventured to say a word about Midwinter or his wife to *me*.

DR. D. (*aside*).

The deuce he didn't! If she discovers that, I lose my last hold on her. (*To* ALLAN.) Are you sure of what you say?

ALLAN.

Quite sure. What *can* have become of Midwinter? I wanted to see him, and say good-bye.

DR. D.

Going away?

ALLAN.

Going to Thorpe-Ambrose by the next train.

DR. D.

In a hurry to get home!

ALLAN.

No, no! In a hurry to see Miss Milroy.

DR. D. (*aside*).

Miss Milroy? I've got it! (*To* ALLAN, *with sudden gravity*.) Let me save you a useless journey. Miss Milroy is not at Thorpe-Ambrose.

ALLAN.

Not at Thorpe-Ambrose ? Where is she ?

DR. D.

Under my care.

ALLAN.

Ill !

DR. D.

A nervous derangement. The newspapers reported you drowned, and Miss Milroy saw the report.

ALLAN.

My darling Neelie ! Under your care ? Do you mean in your house ?

DR. D.

In my Sanatorium at Hendon.

ALLAN.

Let's go there directly !

DR. D.

Contrary to the rules !

ALLAN.

Don't say that ! Stretch a point for once, Doctor !

DR. D.

If I give way, will you be guided by *me?*

ALLAN.

Willingly ! What am I to do ?

DR. D.

Take a cab, drive as far as the turnpike on the road to Hendon, and wait there till I join you.

ALLAN.

How long shall you be ?

DR. D.

If you go at once, not ten minutes after *you.*

ALLAN. '

Thank you a thousand times ! I won't lose a moment !

(*He hurries out.*)

DR. D. (*alone*).

The trap has caught him. Once in my Sanatorium, Mr. Armadale, get out of it if you can ! (*He goes to the door on the right.*) The visitor has gone. I want to speak to you.

(MISS G. *appears at the door.*)

MISS G.

Who has been here ?

DR. D.

Armadale has been here.

MISS G. (*to herself, with concentrated energy*).

Oh, if wishing it could only kill that man ! (*To* DR. D.) What have you done with him ?

DR. D.

I have sent him to my Sanatorium.

MISS G.

What for ?

DR. D.

Can't you guess ?

MISS G.

Can't you tell me ?

DR. D.

I prefer showing you, my fair friend. Have you any particular reason for wishing to stay in these lodgings ?

MISS G.

Stay here ? My husband may be in London ; he may trace me to this house ; he may discover me in my widow's weeds. Take me away ! Anywhere you like, so long as you hide me from my husband's eyes !

DR. D.

Put on your bonnet. (*She goes to put on her bonnet;* DR. D. *continues, watching her satirically.*) Ah ! even under these trying circumstances, there's a melancholy pleasure in putting on a new bonnet ! Let me assist you with your cloak. Is that right ? Very good ! You wish to know what I am going to do with Armadale ? (*He offers his arm. The centre door is suddenly and softly opened.* MIDWINTER *appears on the threshold.*) Come and see !

(*They turn to go out, and discover* MIDWINTER. MISS G. *stands horror-struck.* DR. D. *draws back from her and takes off his hat, bowing to* MIDWINTER, *who stands between them, facing his wife in her widow's weeds.*)

MID. (*with bitter irony*).

Captain Manuel was not to blame, Madam. Captain Manuel did his best to drown me.

(*A pause.*)

DR. D. (*to* MISS G.).

My child, do you understand this gentleman ?

MISS G. (*speaking mechanically*).

No.

MID.

My language shall be plainer. (*To* MISS G.) You are Captain Manuel's accomplice. You were Captain Manuel's mistress before you married *me.* (*He advances a step nearer to her.* DR. D. *starts.*) You need be under no alarm, Sir. She is safe in my loathing and contempt. (MISS G. *lifts her head for the first time, stung by the words.* MID. *proceeds.*) There is one of your old love letters! Further falsehood is hopeless. (*He offers her the letter. She remains motionless, refusing to take it.* MIDWINTER *points to* DR. D.) Leave that man, and follow me!

(*He leads the way to the door.* DR. D. *crosses to* MISS G., *and speaks to her aside.*)

DR. D.

You have his own word for it—he loathes and despises you.

MID. (*at the door*).

Do you hear me?

DR. D. (*aside to* MISS G.).

Say what I say. (*He prompts her.*) You have no right to claim any control over me.

MISS G. (*mechanically repeating the words, in a sinking voice*).
You have no right to claim any control over me.

MID. (*returning a few steps from the door*).
No right? Are you, or are you not, my wife?

DR. D. (*aside to* MISS G.).
One more effort!

MID. (*repeating the question*).
Are you, or are you not, my wife? Yes or No?

MISS G. (*her voice sinking to a whisper*).
No!

(MIDWINTER *advances on her furiously, with a cry of indignation. She shows no fear of him.* DOCTOR DOWNWARD *springs forward to place himself between them.* MIDWINTER *instantly checks himself, and turns sternly to the* DOCTOR.)

MID.

She stands in no need of your protection, sir. I tell you again, she is safe in my loathing and contempt. Let her live in her infamy! I leave her for ever.

(*He leaves the room.* DOCTOR DOWNWARD *looks at* MISS GWILT. *She has neither moved nor spoken since she has disowned her husband. The* DOCTOR *cautiously touches her arm, and speaks in an under tone.*)

DR. D.

Remember Armadale!

(*She rouses herself with a heavy sigh, and slowly looks round at him. He gently puts her arm in his, and speaks again in the same under tone.*)

DR. D.

Come to the Sanatorium.

THE END OF THE FOURTH ACT.

F

ACT. V.

Scene :—*The Sanatorium. The stage represents a drawing-room, with a door and a window at the back, and a bedroom on the right hand. The bedroom is furnished with a bed (without curtains), a table, and a chair. A candle (made to burn gas) is placed on the table. The bedroom is divided from the drawing-room by a vertical partition, with a door in it marked in large characters, on the drawing-room side, No. 1. On the left hand is a similar door, opposite, supposed to lead into another bedroom which is not seen, and marked No. 2. On the drawing-room side of the door of No. 1, and placed close against the partition wall, is a pedestal in imitation marble, with a vase of flowers placed on it. The pedestal is hollow; it opens at the top on the vase being removed, and is supposed to contain the* Doctor's *vaporising apparatus.*

At the rise of the curtain Dr. Downward *and* Allan *are discovered in the drawing-room drinking tea. A moderator lamp on the table, also writing materials. Time—night.*

ALLAN.
Tell me, Doctor, are you quite sure I can't see Miss Milroy ?

DR. D.
Miss Milroy has retired for the night.

ALLAN.
Why, it's barely eleven o'clock !

DR. D.
My good sir, eleven is late in this house. Ten is our hour. After ten I prescribe silence and sleep in the largest doses. By day or night quiet is my grand remedy. All noises die on the threshold of my Sanatorium. Find a door banging in this house if you can ! Discover barking dogs, crowing cocks, hammering workmen, screeching children, here, and I close this establishment to-morrow !

ALLAN.
Can I see Miss Milroy in the morning, early ?

DR. D.
The earlier the better. We are the children of Nature here. When Nature gets up, *we* get up. We rise with the sun, we sing

with the birds, we grow with the grass; and then we go in to breakfast. A pastoral breakfast, Mr. Armadale: milk and honey —milk and honey!

ALLAN.

A drop of brandy wouldn't hurt that pastoral breakfast of yours, Doctor.

DR. D.

Brandy? My young friend, alcohol is poison. I belong to the Temperance League—I believe in nothing but water! (ALLAN *rises, and takes his hat.*) You are not going?

ALLAN.

" Early to bed, and early to rise," Doctor! The instant Miss Milroy goes out to-morrow morning I mean to be in your garden to meet her. I must get a bed somewhere. Is there an hotel at this place?

DR. D.

There is nothing but a public-house.

ALLAN.

Can I get a cab to take me back to London?

DR. D.

There isn't such a thing as a cab in the whole village.

ALLAN.

A pleasant prospect for me! I say, Doctor, I wish you would let me stop here to-night.

DR. D. (*aside*).

He has come to it at last! (*To* ALLAN.) Contrary to the rules, Mr. Armadale.

ALLAN.

Relax the rules for once.

DR. D. (*smiling*).

Mr. Armadale, you possess the gift of persuasion. And you take advantage of it!

ALLAN.

I won't give any trouble. Leave me here for the night, in this comfortable armchair.

DR. D.

My dear Sir, I can't leave you to pass the night in a chair! The hospitality of the Sanatorium is not quite as meagre as that. (*Pointing to the bedroom doors on each side.*) There are two empty bedrooms at your disposal. Which will you have?

ALLAN.

Which is the nearest to Miss Milroy?

DR. D.

Aha, you rogue! Well, well—I should have been like you at

F 2

your age. (*Pointing to No. 1.*)   That is the nearest of the two rooms.

ALLAN.

Then that is the room for me.   (*Looking at his watch.*)   Not twelve yet !   I wish I could annihilate the next five hours.   Do you allow smoking, Doctor ?

DR. D.

Smoking?   Tobacco is poison !   I belong to the Anti-Tobacco League.

ALLAN.

More Leagues ?   What *is* a League, Doctor ?

DR. D.

A League is an Association for forcing *my* ideas down *your* throat.   It is the natural offspring of a free country.

ALLAN.

Do you think the League would discover me if I went out and smoked in the garden ?

DR. D.

See what it is to be the slave of a bad habit !   Go into the garden, my young friend.   You will be physically the worse for the tobacco, but you will be morally the better after contemplating the stars !

ALLAN.

Six of one and half-a-dozen of the other—eh ?   (*He takes out his cigar case.*)   I should be perfectly happy now if it wasn't for one thing.

DR. D.

Any anxiety that I can remove ?

ALLAN.

I can't help thinking of poor Midwinter.

DR. D.

Do you suppose your absence will alarm him ?

ALLAN.

No fear of that.   He knows where I am.

DR. D. (*aside*).

The devil he does !

ALLAN (*choosing a cigar*).

I stopped at the hotel and left a note for him as I went by It's an old engagement of mine with Midwinter never to leave him without telling him where to find me.   He's under a delusion, poor fellow, that I shall do something rash one of these days, and that he is to be the means of saving me.   (*Putting on his hat.*) How shall I find my way to the garden ?

DR. D.

The servant will show you. No noise, mind!

ALLAN.

Oh, no noise! I'll be as silent as the grave. (*Exit.*)

DR. D. (*alone*).

"As silent as the grave"? You may find, Mr. Armadale, that we interpret your metaphor literally in this house! (*He takes a turn backwards and forwards thoughtfully.*) He's young, he's strong: there isn't a lurking morsel of disease about him to account for his death. And, to make matters worse, Midwinter knows he is here. (MISS GWILT *enters by the drawing-room door. The* DOCTOR *observes her.*) My dear child, how rash! Armadale has just left me; he might have seen you on the stairs.

MISS G. (*calmly*).

He has not seen me. Have you let him go?

DR. D.

Have I taken leave of my senses? He has gone to smoke in the garden. At his own request he stays here for the night. (*Pointing to it.*) He sleeps in that room.

MISS G. (*noticing the tea things*).

Has he been drinking tea with you?

DR. D.

Yes.

MISS G. (*taking up* ALLAN'S *empty cup*).

Have you poisoned him?

DR. D.

Poisoned him? Poison leaves traces, my dear, and coroners' inquests sit on people who die mysteriously. Any more questions?

MISS G. (*maintaining the tone of impenetrable composure in which she has spoken thus far*).

One more. You have written a letter to Armadale's executors, falsely declaring me to be Armadale's widow, and falsely claiming the widow's income. Can the law reach you for doing that?

DR. D.

Yes, if Armadale says the word.

MISS G. (*suddenly advancing on* DR. D.).

Armadale dies to-night, or *I* say the word!

DR. D.

You!

MISS G. (*beginning to lose her self-control*).

Take your choice! You smooth-tongued villain, take your choice!

DR. D. (*drawing back*).

She has lost her senses!

MISS G.

She has *found* her senses! She has mastered her master at last. There is a danger you never bargained for in trampling down to your level a woman like me. She sees you with *your* eyes—she judges you with *your* cunning—and she ends in knowing you for what you are! From first to last I have been a means of getting money, moved by your merciless hands. My life has been wasted—my heart has been turned to stone—my tongue has been taught to lie—I have loved and hoped—I have sinned and suffered—to put money in *your* pocket. Are you to profit by the loss of everything that made love noble and life dear to me? And am I to be flung off like the glove that you have worn out? I stand here, in the horror of my degradation, with nothing to hope and nothing to fear more; and I tell you to your face, if you are to have the widow's income, as true as there is a heaven above us you shall earn it first!

DR. D.

One word, before your frenzy carries you farther!

MISS G.

My frenzy! Who fed my frenzy? You! What did you say to me before my husband came in? "If you own Midwinter now, you submit to be treated by him like the most abandoned woman living. Thanks to Armadale—remember that!" Those were your own words.

DR. D.

Let me speak! I have seen Armadale since. Believe me, I was mistaken, and you were mistaken.

MISS G.

Believe you? He is one incarnate lie from head to foot, and he asks me to believe him! Who divided my husband's love with me, when I *had* a husband? Armadale! Who suspected my past life, and talked of secrets and mysteries before me in my husband's presence? Armadale! Who hired Manuel, and brought him into the house? Who took my husband away to sea, and told him my miserable secret? Armadale! The rapture of being revenged on him leaps through me like fire! His life! his life! Give me Armadale's life, and hang me before all London to-morrow!

DR. D.

You will rouse the house! On my knees—on my knees— I entreat you to be quiet!

MISS G. (*looking down at him with a burst of triumph*).

Ah! you know your place at last! (*A knock is heard at the door.*)

DR. D. (*hastily seating himself*).

Who's there?

A VOICE OUTSIDE.

Francis, sir.

DR. D. (*to* MISS G.).

Compose yourself. It's only the night attendant. (*Calling.*) Come in! (FRANCIS *enters.*) What do you want?

FRANCIS.

The head nurse sent me here, sir. The lady in room No. 10 is worse than ever. It's asthma; and every breath she draws seems likely to be her last.

DR. D. (*impatiently*).

Tell the nurse to medicate the air in the room, and the patient's asthma will be relieved. If she has not got the right mixture— (*he points to the pedestal*)—take off the flowers, and see if the bottle isn't there.

(FRANCIS *puts the flowers on a side table, lifts the top of the pedestal, which opens back with a hinge, takes out a chemical bottle from the inside, and shows it to the* DOCTOR. MISS GWILT *watches* FRANCIS *with sudden curiosity from the moment when he lifts the cover of the pedestal.*)

FRANCIS.

Right, sir?

DR. D. (*impatiently*).

Quite right.

(FRANCIS *goes out.* MISS GWILT *approaches the mock pedestal and looks in.*

MISS G.

Why is your apparatus hidden in this thing?

DR. D. (*more and more irritably*).

My apparatus is a common earthenware jar. I can't have such a thing seen in a drawing-room. The pedestal is orna-mental, and I put the jar in the pedestal.

MISS G.

Why is the pedestal outside the bedroom instead of in?

DR. D. (*always answering irritably until he discovers the real object of* MISS G.'s *questions*).

What do these idle questions mean?

MISS G.

More than you suppose. Answer me.

DR. D.

I have nervous, unreasonable people to deal with. If they saw the Vaporizer being charged they might fancy I was suffocating them.

MISS G. (*thoughtfully*).

Suffocating them ? Go on.

DR. D.

Go on ? Were we talking of these trifling things when Francis came in ?

MISS G.

My questions have a motive. (*Placing her hand on the pedestal.*) The vapour is made here ? What next ?

DR. D.

The vapour, as you call it, is conveyed to the patient inside by means of a pipe in the wall.

MISS G.

A patient suffering from asthma ?

DR. D.

From asthma, from consumption, from other diseases which can be reached by the lungs. The relief in some cases, the cure in others, is obtained by different ways of medicating the air in the room. Are you satisfied now?

MISS G.

I have a last question to ask. You put this Vaporizer to a use that cures. Could you put it to a use that kills?

DR. D. (*starting to his feet*).

What ! ! !

MISS G.

Could you poison the air in that room ?

DR. D. (*controlling himself*).

Chemistry can poison anything. (*Aside, walking away from* MISS G.). Amazing that I should never have thought of it myself !

MISS G. (*standing by the pedestal*).

Dr. Downward !

DR. D. (*pursuing his reflections*).

My knowledge labours, and sees nothing but the difficulty and the risk ; her ignorance guesses, and hits the mark !

MISS G.

Dr. Downward ! (DR. D. *turns to her.*) See if Armadale is still in the garden.

(DR. D. *goes to the window, raises it softly, and looks out. While he is thus occupied* MISS G. *hurriedly writes a few lines at the side table, folds and directs the note.   The* DOCTOR *returns.*)

DR. D.
Armadale is walking up and down, smoking his cigar. (MISS G. *rings the bell at the side of the drawing-room fireplace.*)   What are you ringing for ?

MISS G.
I am ringing for Francis.

DR. D.
Why ?

MISS G.
When Francis comes in, one of us must give him an order. Either *you* send him for what chemistry wants to poison the air in that room, or *I* send him with this note to Armadale in the garden.   (*She shows him what she has written.   A knock is heard at the door.*)   Shall I speak, or will you ?

DR. D. (*resuming his usual smooth manner*).
I wouldn't give you the trouble of speaking for the world ! Come in.

(FRANCIS *enters.*)

FRANCIS.
Did you ring, Sir ?

DR. D.
Yes.   (*Gives him a key.*)   Go into the dispensary, and open the third cupboard from the door.   You will find a leather bag in it, and a small mahogany chest.   Bring me the bag and the chest, and at the same time let me have a bottle of water.

(FRANCIS *goes out.*)

MRS. G. (*lighting her note at the lamp, and throwing it into the fire-place*).
You see ?

DR. D.
A thousand thanks !   I see !

(*A momentary pause.   MISS G. seats herself with her back to the DOCTOR, and speaks aside.*)

MISS G.
The silence maddens me !   I must speak—even to *him*.   (*To DR. D., without looking at him.*)   Is it a fine night ?

DR. D. (*answering, without looking at MISS G.*).
There isn't a cloud in the sky anywhere.

MISS G. (*looking round impatiently towards the door*).
How long the man is !

DR. D. (*looking round also*).
Francis is slower than ever to-night.

MISS G. (*to* DR. D.).

You are very quiet here.

DR. D.

We are very quiet here.

MISS G.

Are they building in the neighbourhood ?

DR. D.

Yes, but not within our hearing.

MISS G.

In a few years more Hendon will be a suburb of London.

DR. D.

I suppose so.

(*Enter* FRANCIS *with the chest. He is followed by a man servant with the bag and the bottle of water, who waits at the door until* FRANCIS *has relieved him of what he carries.* FRANCIS *places the things on the table.*)

FRANCIS.

Will that do, sir ?

DR. D.

That will do. (FRANCIS *goes out. The* DOCTOR *addresses* MISS G.) You insist ?

MISS G. (*rising*).

I insist.

DR. D.

Be so obliging as to hold something for me. (*Taking the bag in one hand, he puts the other into the hollow of the pedestal, produces a large circular cork with a hole in the centre, and a glass funnel, and gives them to* MISS G. *to hold.*)

DR. D.

The cork stops the mouth of the jar inside. The funnel receives the liquid to be poured in, without troubling to remove the jar.

(*He empties the contents of the bag into the jar. The contents are heard to drop, as if many particles of stone were falling on earthenware. The* DOCTOR *next takes the bottle of water, and empties it into the jar. He then replaces the cork and funnel, bowing with scrupulous politeness as he takes them from* MISS G.)

MISS G.

Is it done ?

DR. D.

Not yet. (*He unlocks the chest, aud takes out a chemical bottle, then produces another bottle of the size and shape of a double smelling-bottle, but larger, fills it at both ends from the chemical bottle, which he locks up again in the chest, and addresses* MISS G.) You still insist ?

MISS G.

I still insist.

DR. D. *(giving* MISS G. *the bottle)*.

You see the glass funnel at the mouth of the jar.

MISS G.

I see it.

DR. D.

You see four divisions marked on the bottle that you have in your hand ?

MISS G.

Yes.

DR. D.

Four separate pourings into the funnel, at intervals of five minutes each, and, if Armadale sleeps in that room, Armadale dies at the fourth pouring.

MISS G.

Suddenly ?

DR. D.

Slowly. And if the doctors examine him after death, all they can discover is that he has died of apoplexy or of congestion of the lungs.

MISS G.

What if he wakes ?

DR. D.

If he wakes he sees nothing, he smells nothing, he feels nothing but a sense of oppression and a desire to sleep again. Are you satisfied ?

MISS G.

I am satisfied.

DR. D. *(closing the top of the pedestal, and putting the vase of flowers back on it)*.

Retire at once, before Armadale comes in. (FRANCIS *enters hurriedly.*) What do you want ?

FRANCIS.

I beg your pardon, Sir. There is a stranger at the garden gate.

(MISS G. *starts, and looks at the* DR.)

DR. D. *(to* FRANCIS).

Have you let the person in ?

FRANCIS.

No, Sir. But Mr. Armadale——

DR. D

Has Mr. Armadale seen him ?

FRANCIS.

Mr. Armadale is talking to him through the rails of the gate.

DR. D. (*resignedly*).

Let the gentleman in.

(FRANCIS *goes out.*)

MISS G. (*in sudden terror*).

My husband ?

DR. D.

Your husband. There is no help for it. We must either rouse Armadale's suspicion, or open the gate. Run upstairs again before they come here. Quick, or your husband will see you !

MISS G. (*resolutely*).

One word first. Come what may of my husband surprising us, if you hurt a hair of his head——

DR. D.

What ! Fond of him still ?

MISS G.

If you hurt a hair of his head——

DR. D.

Trust me to run no risks. He shall go out as safely as he came in. (*He opens the drawing-room door.* MISS G. *hurries out. The* DR. *returns to the front.*) Where is the way out of it *now* ? If I put Midwinter's safety in peril there's no knowing what his wife's frenzy may do. If I leave him to act as he pleases, I leave him to snatch Armadale's life out of our hands !

(*Enter* ALLAN *and* MIDWINTER, *arm in arm.*

ALLAN.

Here we are, Doctor ! Midwinter owes you every apology for this late visit ; and I owe you a world of thanks for letting him in, because he is my friend.

DR. D. (*politely*).

What is the object of Mr. Midwinter's visit ?

MID.

My object is ˌto remove Mr. Armadale instantly from your house.

ALLAN (*aside to* DR. D.).

Don't notice what he says. Something seems to have upset him—he's out of sorts.

DR. D. (*to* MIDWINTER).

Just as you please, Sir. The decision rests with Mr. Armadale, not with me. (*He retires, and seats himself at the back, watching* ALLAN *and* MID.)

ALLAN (*to* MID.).

I told you you would find it all right, if you only saw the doctor yourself!

MID.

And *I* told *you* that the doctor's word was not to be relied on.

ALLAN.

Hush ! hush ! he may hear you.

MID.

He has lied in telling you Miss Milroy is here.   He has some underhand motive for getting you into the house.

ALLAN.

How can you talk so ! He has received you, just as he received me, in the friendliest manner.

(*Enter* FRANCIS.)

FRANCIS (*to* MID.).

The cabman wishes to know, Sir, if he is to wait ?

DR. D. (*rising, and coming forward*).

Well, Mr. Armadale, do you go with your friend ?

ALLAN.

Go all the way back to London ? and then come all the way back here, before six to-morrow ? No, no, doctor ; I am not quite so foolish as that !

MID. (*giving money to* FRANCIS).

There is the cabman's money.   He may go.

(FRANCIS *goes out.*)

DR. D.

Without you ?

MID.

Without me. (*The* DOCTOR *and* ALLAN *both start.*   MID. *proceeds with bitter irony.*) You are a medical man. Perhaps you can tell me if my troubles have affected my mind ?   I mean to stay here to-night with my friend, and I don't expect you to raise the smallest objection to it.   Am I labouring under an insane delusion, Dr. Downward ?

DR. D. (*with a low bow, making the best of it*).

You are welcome to the Sanatorium, Mr. Midwinter. Stay here with your friend by all means.

(*He turns to go out.* ALLAN *follows and speaks to him.*)

ALLAN.

Doctor, I am really ashamed——

DR. D.

Don't mention it ! (*He touches his forehead.*) Your friend's case is worth studying.

ALLAN (*alarmed*).

You don't mean it !

DR. D.

I do ! Excuse me for one moment. I must tell the servant that your friend sleeps here.

(*He goes out.*)

MID.

Allan ! (ALLAN *returns to him.*) Will you consent to put my opinion of Dr. Downward and your opinion to a plain test ? Where is your bedroom ?

ALLAN (*pointing to* No. 1).

There.

MID. (*crossing to the opposite door*).

Is this a bedroom ?

ALLAN.

An empty bedroom. I had my choice of that or the other.

MID.

An empty bedroom. Now, mark my words ! When Dr. Downward comes back, you will find that my room is in another part of the house, and you will hear the Doctor make some excuse to prevent me from sleeping there.

(*He points to* No. 2.)

ALLAN (*aside*).

Oh, dear ! oh, dear !

(*Enter* DR. D.)

DR. D.

Your room will be ready in ten minutes, Mr. Midwinter.

MID.

Where do I sleep ?

DR. D.

On the other side of the house.

MID. (*to* ALLAN).

What did I tell you ?

DR. D. (*aside, observing* MID.).

I have made a false move !

MID. (*opening the door of* No. 2).

Why on the other side of the house, when there is an empty room here ?

DR. D. (*aside*).

I see !

MID.

You had forgotten this room, I suppose ?

DR. D.

Totally !

MID.

I wish to sleep here, opposite my friend.

DR. D. (*with a bow*).

Sleep there by all means ! I have not the shadow of an objection to it.

ALLAN (*ironically to* MID.).

Still doubtful of the Doctor ?

MID. (*turning away*).

No. Sure of him now !

DR. D.

Can I offer you any refreshment, gentlemen ? No ? I will ring for the servant then. (*He rings.* FRANCIS *enters.*) Light the candles, Francis, in No. 1 and No. 2. (FRANCIS *enters* No. 1, *and lights the gas candle on the table. The* DOCTOR *continues.*) Francis will take your instructions, gentlemen, for calling you in the morning.

(DR. D. *retires to the back of the drawing-room.* ALLAN *addresses* FRANCIS *as he comes out of the door of* No. 1.)

ALLAN (*to* FRANCIS).

Is it your business to call us in the morning ?

FRANCIS.

The day attendant calls you, Sir. I write his orders overnight on the slate.

ALLAN (*pointing to* No. 1).

This is my room. Write that I am to be called at six tomorrow morning.

FRANCIS (*writing*).

" Mr. Armadale—room No. 1—to be called at six." (*He turns to* MIDWINTER.) Any orders, sir ?

MID.

No orders.

(FRANCIS *enters the room numbered* " 2." DR. D. *returns to* ALLAN *and* MIDWINTER.)

DR. D.

Good night, gentlemen.

ALLAN.

Good night, Doctor !

(*He goes into room* No. 1. MID. *follows him in, and, after first closing the door of communication, carefully examines the room,*

and notices that the key is on the inner side of the door. ALLAN
observes him with astonishment. As the door closes on them
FRANCIS *comes out of* No. 2. *The* DOCTOR *speaks to him.*)

DR. D.

Wait a little, Francis, before you turn out the lamp in the
drawing-room. (FRANCIS *waits at the back.* DR. D. *takes the
key out of the lock of* No. 2, *and continues, speaking to himself.*) If
you *will* sleep opposite your friend, Mr. Midwinter, we must
keep you within the limits of your own room. (*He looks towards
the door of* No. 1.) When is he coming out?

ALLAN (*watching* MIDWINTER'S *examination of his room*).
My dear fellow, what *does* this mean?

MID.

Wait till the morning, and I'll tell you. In the meantime,
lock your door.

(*He returns to the drawing-room, closing* ALLAN'S *door.* ALLAN
seats himself on the side of the bed, and falls into thought. MID.
meets the DOCTOR *face to face, looks at him steadily, and
speaks quietly, as if thinking aloud.*)

MID.

You were in league with my wife this afternoon, and you
have entrapped my friend into your house to-night. Is there
any connection between the outrage you have offered to *me* and
the snare you have set for *him?*

DR. D.

Do you expect me to answer that question?

MID.

I expect the night to answer it.

(*He goes into his room and closes the door.*)

DR. D. (*alone*).

I'll keep you waiting for the answer! (*He approaches the door
with the key in his hand, and checks himself.*) No! Let me give
him time to fall asleep first. (*He speaks to* FRANCIS.) Turn
down the lamp, Francis; but be careful not to turn it quite out
to-night. I may want to come back.

(*He goes out.* FRANCIS *turns down the lamp. The drawing-room
is obscured; but the bedroom No. 1 is still lit by the candle.*
ALLAN *remains seated on the side of the bed.* FRANCIS, *leaving
the lamp, advances softly to the front, takes a slip of paper out
of his waistcoat pocket, and looks hesitatingly at the door of*
No. 2.)

FRANCIS.

How had I better give this to Mr. Midwinter? I'll slip it
under his **door.**

(*He pushes the paper under* MIDWINTER'S *door, and softly leaves the drawing-room. After a short pause* MIDWINTER *opens the door with the paper in his hand, and looks about the empty drawing-room.*)

MID.

Nobody in the room! Who *can* have slipped this under my door? Is it really meant for me? (*He turns the lamp up a little higher, and reads by the light of it.*) "Sir,—This comes to you from an unknown friend. I have been instructed to watch the Doctor's house, and I heard what you said to Mr. Armadale at the gate. Others are interested in him besides you. Major and Miss Milroy are in London, and the young lady has persuaded her father to consult his lawyer——" (*He pauses, and speaks.*) Proof, if proof was needed, that Miss Milroy is *not* in the house! (*He goes on reading.*) "The upshot of it is that we are going to take the Doctor for debt, on the chance of fixing him afterwards with a serious offence against the law. We have squared Francis, who will let us into the house. I have sent a messenger to Major Milroy, to tell him you and Mr. Armadale are here. Keep an eye on your friend, and wait till we come." It may be hours before they come! and what may not happen in that time? Has Allan taken the common precaution of locking his door? (*He puts the slip of paper into his breast pocket, advances to the door of No. 1, and checks himself.*) Stop! Let me look at my own door first. (*He opens his door, and notices the absence of the key.*) No key! It's plain I am to be locked in. (*He pauses to reflect.*) Let me think! The Doctor waited, and saw Allan into *his* room; waited again, and saw *me* into *mine*. If I can do nothing else, I can baffle the villain's calculations, and I will! (*He crosses, and knocks at* ALLAN'S *door.*) Are you in bed? (ALLAN *rises and opens the door.*) What, not undressed yet?

ALLAN (*smiling*).

I didn't think of it. I can think of nothing but Miss Milroy.

MID.

Will you humour me for the last time? Let us change rooms.

ALLAN.

Why?

MID.

I have taken a liking to your room.

ALLAN.

Nonsense! One room is as good as the other.

MID.

Very likely. But there is a difference in the beds.

ALLAN.

What difference?

MID.

My bed has got curtains, and your bed has none. I can't
sleep comfortably with curtains round me.

ALLAN (*yielding*).

All right! Take my bed, you old fidget, and I will take
yours! Will *that* quiet you?

MID.

That will quiet me, Allan. Good night.

(*They shake hands.* ALLAN *enters* No. 2, *and closes the door.*
MID. *waits to see him safe into the room, and then locks himself
into* No. 1.)

MID. (*in* No. 1).

Can I do more than I have done? (*He listens.*) Not a sound
stirring, indoors or out! (*He seats himself by a little table in the
room.*) Has the day of atonement dawned for me at last? Is
Allan's life to be saved to-night, and saved by *me*? If I could
only know how soon the men will be here! Is there no hint
to guide me in the warning I read just now? (*He takes out the
paper, and with it another letter in the same pocket. He looks
through the paper and puts it back with a gesture in the negative;
then takes up and opens the letter.*) Oh, me! a note from my wife,
in the first days of our marriage—in the golden time of our
love! Who would believe that the woman who wrote these
charming lines and the woman who has deceived and disgraced
me are one? (*His left hand closes mechanically on the letter. His
right hand supports his head as he sits thinking by the table. The
door of the drawing-room opens, and* FRANCIS *appears with a candle,
followed by* MISS GWILT. *The ensuing scene, and* MISS G'S *scene
which follows, must be played in undertones until the moment when*
MISS G. *discovers* MIDWINTER.)

FRANCIS.

The housemaid will have your room ready for you, ma'am,
in a quarter of an hour. No. 7, at the end of the corridor.

MISS G.

Why can't I have one of these rooms?

FRANCIS (*turning up the lamp a little higher*).

They are occupied by the two gentlemen who came here this
evening. (*Pointing to* No. 1.) Mr. Armadale is in that room.

MISS G. (*as if doubting* FRANCIS).

Mr. Armadale? I thought he was on the floor above us.

FRANCIS.

I have got it down on the slate, ma'am, by the gentleman's own orders. (*He shows the slate.*) " Mr. Armadale, room No. 1, to be called at six."

MISS G. (*aside*).

Armadale is there !

(FRANCIS (*pointing to* No. 2).

The other gentleman on this side is Mr. Midwinter. (MISS G. *starts.*) If you don't object to waiting here, ma'am, the housemaid will come to show you the way to your room.

MISS G. (*with her eyes fixed on the door of* No. 2).

Tell the housemaid I shall not want her. I know the way.

FRANCIS.

I wish you good night, ma'am.

MISS G. (*as before*).

Good night. (FRANCIS *goes out, taking his candle with him.* MISS G. *approaches nearer to the door of* No. 2, *and speaks in low, suppressed tones.*) He is there !—there, within a few yards of me—the husband whose right I have denied, whose love I have lost for ever ! (*She produces the bottle which the* DOCTOR *gave her.*) Should I rouse some nobler feeling in him than contempt if he saw me now, with his friend's life in my hands ?

(*The* DOCTOR *enters softly with the key of* No. 2. *The dialogue between them is carried on in whispers.*)

DR. D. (*after listening at the door of No.* 1).

All quiet ! Not a sound stirring in the room. (*He softly approaches the door of* No. 2.)

MISS G. (*stopping him*).

What are you about ?

DR. D.

I'm going to lock him in.

MISS G.

No !

DR. D.

Why not ?

MISS G.

It's an insult to lock him in. He shall suffer insult no more from you or me. Go ! (*She points to the drawing room door, then turns aside and removes the vase of flowers from the pedestal. While she does this the* DOCTOR *listens at the keyhole of* No. 2.)

DR. D. (*aside*).

No need of the key—he is asleep. (*Rises, and speaks to* MISS G., *who returns to him.*) No noise ! Whatever you do, my dear, no noise !

MISS G.

Leave me! (*Looking at him with contempt.*) You are trembling.

DR. D.

Am I? (*He puts his finger on his pulse.*) Quicker than usual, by Jupiter! (*He goes out.*)

MISS G. (*holding up the bottle*).

Four pourings from this and the poisoned air steals in and fills the fatal room. (*She advances to* No. 1, *and lifts the cover of the pedestal.*) Die, you who have divided my husband with me! Die, you who have made me the woman I am! (*She drops the first pouring into the funnel, then draws an easy chair close to the pedestal, seats herself, and looks at her watch, then fixes her eyes on the door of* No. 2.) Is he sleeping? Is he waking? Is he thinking of *me*? Oh, the dreadful stillness! Even the wind in the garden is dead to-night. (*She rises and pushes her hair back.*) Something throbs and burns in my head. My hair— how clinging and heavy my hair is to-night! (*She returns to the pedestal after another look at her watch.*) The minutes are counted out—the interval is past! Will it be easier the second time than the first? (*She pours again from the bottle—pauses, shuddering—then puts the bottle down upon the table.*) Two more intervals to pass!

(*A long pause. She remains standing by the table. The candle, still alight in room No. 1, begins to grow dim. MIDWINTER, who has hitherto sat motionless, as if sinking into sleep from fatigue, now stirs in his chair mechanically.*)

MID. (*to himself, in low, faint tones*).

How heavy the air is to-night! (*His head sinks on his breast, his eyes close. MISS GWILT looks at her watch, and speaks once more.*)

MISS G.

The minutes stand still—the silence petrifies the restless time! Nothing moves but the chill that creeps over me— nothing sounds but the fever throbbing in my head!

(*The flame of the candle in MIDWINTER'S room sinks lower. MIDWINTER moves again. He notices the waning light, half rises, drops back again into the chair, rises again, holding by the table; looks wildly round him, and cries out faintly.*)

MID.

Allan!

MISS G. (*just hearing the cry*).

Who calls "Allan"? (*She looks at* No. 2, *then glances back again at* No. 1.) Armadale is here!

(MIDWINTER *reaches the door, supports himself against it with one hand, and feels with the other for the key. He rallies his failing strength, and calls again, "* ALLAN !")

MISS G.

My husband's voice! God in heaven! they have changed rooms. (*She tries to force in the locked door.*) Turn the key! the lock! the lock! (MIDWINTER, *by a last effort, finds the key in the lock, turns it, half opens the door, and falls forward insensible into his wife's arms. Remaining by the door, she places him in the easy chair which stands near the pedestal, and supports his head on her bosom. She feels the poisoned air coming from the room.*)

MISS G.

The poisoned air! It will kill him in my arms! (*She closes the door, looks at* MIDWINTER *again, and places her hand on his heart.*) Dead? No! I feel a fluttering at his heart. What is this in his hand? (*She opens* MIDWINTER'S *left hand and finds the letter, on which his fingers have remained mechanically closed.*) My letter! my letter, written to him in the first days of our marriage! Oh, my husband, was there a little corner in your heart still left for me? How can I be grateful for the love that has not quite forgotten me, even yet! There is one way, and but one! I can free him from me for ever! (*She stoops over him and kisses his forehead.*) The last kiss, love!—a dying woman has that privilege, even when she is a wretch like me! (*She rests* MIDWINTER'S *head on the back of the chair, and takes the bottle from the table.*) The one atonement I can make to him is the atonement of my death. (*She pours the whole contents of the bottle into the funnel, and returns to* MIDWINTER.) Oh, he lives! he looks at me!

MID. (*faintly*).

Allan! (*Recognising his wife.*) You? you here?

MISS G.

You have saved Armadale, and you have saved him from *me*. Ask no more. (*She knocks at the door of* No. 2. MIDWINTER'S *head sinks back again on the chair.*)

ALLAN (*speaking within*).

What is it?

MISS G. (*speaking through the door*).

Your friend wants you. (*She draws back.*)

ALLAN (*opening his door*).

You! (*Turning from* MISS G., *and hurrying to* MIDWINTER.) Good God! Is he dead?

MISS G.

Faint—only faint. Draw him nearer to the window. Give him air.

(ALLAN *draws the chair back a little, then throws up the window; then turns and speaks to* MISS G.)

ALLAN.

Where is the Doctor ?

MISS G.

Don't trust him ! Rouse the house !

(*She crosses to the door of* No. 1, *and prepares to open it.*)

ALLAN (*hurrying to the drawing-room door*).

Help ! help !

(*He goes out.* MIDWINTER, *roused by* ALLAN'S *voice, raises himself feebly in the chair, and sees his wife standing at the door of* No. 1.)

MID.

Lydia !

MISS G. (*with infinite tenderness*).

My name, as he used to speak it ! His last word to me is an echo of the old time ! (*She returns to him and kneels at his feet.*) I am not all bad. Forgive me—and forget me ! Farewell for ever !

(*She enters the room and turns the key in the lock. The next moment the poisoned air overpowers her. She staggers, and drops on the floor. The candle, reduced to its last point of flame, goes out.*)

MID. (*trying vainly to rise*).

Lydia ! Lydia !

(*Voices are heard outside.*)

A MAN'S VOICE.

Dr. Downward !

THE DOCTOR'S VOICE.

Who wants me ?

THE MAN'S VOICE.

You are my prisoner.

ALLAN'S VOICE.

Neelie !

MISS MILROY'S VOICE.

Allan ! Allan !

(MISS MILROY *and* ALLAN *appear together at the drawing-room door. They hasten to* MIDWINTER. *As* ALLAN *bends over him and takes his hand the curtain falls.*)

THE END.